Underland Arcana explores the hidden spaces beneath the stairs and continues to lurk up in the attic. Here are stories about decoding human connections, stories about snakes, stories about what happens when you leave that stain too long, stories about witches, stories about disappearances, and stories about love and loss. These are the stories that creep up on us at night.

Underland Arcana is published quarterly. This issue is published in conjunction with the new moon that slips across the edge of the world and creeps across a new sky.

EDITOR
Mark Teppo

COVER IMAGE
Grandfailure

SIGIL ART
Andrew Penn Romine

PUBLISHER
Underland Press
Clackamas, OR, USA

Hear the whisper and creak of the world around you ...

https://www.underlandarcana.com

UNDERLAND
ARCANA

~ 05 ~

Underland Press

Contents

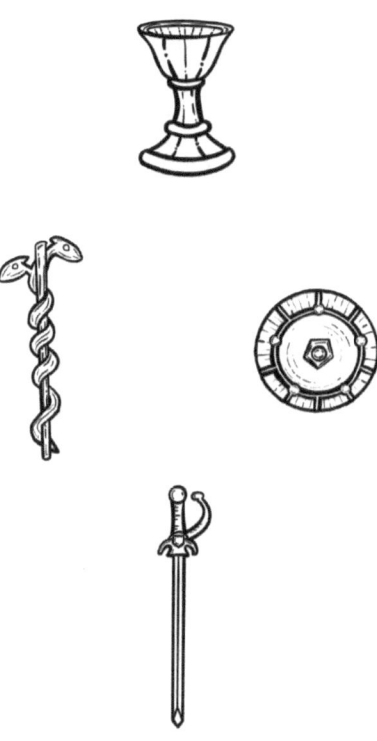

The Lay of the Land

Back in the day, as part of the outlining process, I would do full ten card readings for the characters in my novels. After building the nine-box outline and envisioning the movie trailer beats and letting it all sit for a few days, I would gather a few decks and lay out the cards. I would do the reading with one deck, and then lay out the same reading in a different deck, seeing if one set of images worked better than the other. All the major characters for both *Lightbreaker* and *Heartland* had readings done for them.

It was all about building a vibe. About getting a sense of what these characters wanted to be. Where they wanted to go. What the Universe had in store for them.

I would make notes, maybe even build a graphic of the reading (using the *Vertigo Deck*, because, you know, Dave McKean art and all), and then I would paste it up in my notebook and forget about it. Okay, maybe I would look at it once or twice when I got stuck on the book, but mostly, I let it simmer. Let it soak into the creative loam and sprout.

The cards never tell you the future, after all. They only show you the way. They give you a glimpse of a path. It's up to you to figure out how to get from here to there, or if you even want to go there. It's all very broad stroke and throwing ideas out and seeing what forms.

This is the beginning of what I'm calling "Deck Two," this second year of *Underland Arcana*. I learned some things in this first year—about myself and what I like to read, about what people think of when they try not to consciously write tarot stories. The writers and I have started to shape the *Arcana*, and I'm eager to see where it goes this year. But, for now, I present you with issue 5. This is the one where we hit our stride. Maybe. Or maybe we're still trying to find our way out of the room we locked ourselves in.

And yes, maybe that's a metaphor for where everyone is these days as we navigate this strange world we have found ourselves in. Who knows?

I do know one thing: we're going to keep telling stories, and I hope you keep enjoying them.

Onward!

Mark Teppo
Feb 12th, 2022

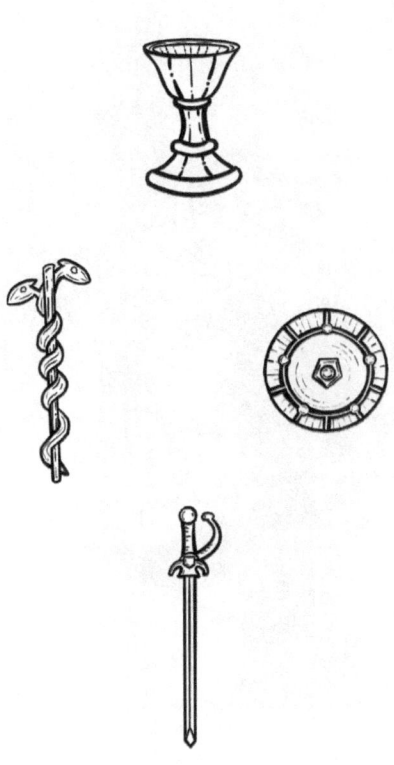

Small Packages

~ *Nina Kiriki Hoffman*

Sarah opened the new box of Cheerios and worked the waxed bag open. Lo and behold, there was a small package inside amongst the honey-nut goodness.

Cereal boxes hadn't had prizes in them in decades, but Sarah lived in hope. She had been waiting twenty-five years for a decoder ring. She couldn't read the messages the aliens sent through her email. She printed them out and kept them in a file folder, waiting for this day.

She snipped off the end of the prize package and shook the prize out onto the turquoise kitchen table of her small condo.

Not a decoder ring. It was a red plastic heart.

Frowning, she opened the heart. It had a message inside: "Meet me at Burrows Coffee Shop at 5:30."

No signature.

She figured aliens would be able to beam a decoder ring into the exact cereal box she had plucked from a wall of cereal boxes at the SuperMart. They knew where to find her.

But no, some rando had put a message in a cereal box, not knowing who was going to open it. Or when. Or where. Had this come from the General Mills factory?

Were they talking about a coffee shop in wherever General Mills was?

There was a Burrows Coffee Shop two blocks from the library where Sarah worked, and she got off at five. Couldn't hurt to drop by. She got coffee there all the time anyway.

She picked up the message and sniffed it. It smelled like lavender, her least favorite essential oil.

Could she like anybody who sent a lavender-scented note?

It was only a day until Valentine's Day. If a boyfriend had sent her a plastic heart, she would wonder. A cheap and easily breakable heart didn't bode well for a relationship. Then again, she'd never even had a boyfriend, so maybe a bad one was better than nothing.

She liked the school-kid Valentines they sold at supermarkets, cartoon characters and superheroes talking about friendship. She bought a package every year to hand out to everybody at the library. She still remembered how sad she'd been in grade school when she only got a Valentine from her best friend Basima, and other people were getting sacks of them. Sarah always bought a Valentine for everybody in her class, but other people didn't.

Everybody should get a little Valentine's magic.

Other people at the library had started passing out kid Valentines, too, following her lead. Basima, who worked at the library too, was the first, but not the only.

Sarah poured out a bowl of Cheerios, added milk, and took a bite. She tucked the message back in the heart and put the heart in her giant green purse, with all the other things she might possibly need in the course of her day —protein bars, a pretend ray gun she sometimes waved at noisy children in the storytelling circle to make them settle down, a first aid kit, a phone charger, a small pad of colored paper so she could write notes to people who mis-behaved, a roll of tape to tape the notes up with, Sharpies, assorted fountain pens, Tampax, her wallet and keys.

She had just rinsed out her cereal bowl when she no-ticed an alien on the kitchen table. It looked like a cock-roach, but its wildly waving antennae were golden, and its wing cases had symbols on them in gold — she rec-ognized the glyphs from the alien emails, which she had studied without success.

"Hello," she said. "I hope you come in peace." She opened the Cheerios box and took out three Cheerios. She put them on the table in front of the bug.

Its metallic antennae waved independently of each other. She wished she knew cockroach or alien sign lan-guage. It fell on the Cheerios and ate them.

She put down five more before she rerolled the bag and closed the box. As much as she longed for alien contact, she didn't want things eating her food before she could.

The roach ate three more Cheerios, then waved its an-tennae and bobbed its head at her. She wasn't sure what that meant. She left the last two Cheerios on the table for the alien to snack on later. "Do you have anything to tell me?" she asked.

The roach bobbed its head.

"Oh! That's interesting! But I don't speak your language, and I have to get to work. Maybe we can work out a code later?"

It bobbed again.

She left it and headed for the library.

After work, she stood in the door of Burrows and looked around. How was she supposed to recognize the person who'd sent her the message?

How likely was it that the message was a prank, and there would never be anyone waiting in a coffee shop for her? About ninety-eight point five percent. Still, Burrows had the best Danish in town. She could get a raspberry Danish and maybe share it with the alien roach when she went home.

Only one person sat at a table. Basima, her best friend. Basima lifted a hand and wiggled fingers at Sarah.

Sarah went to the counter and ordered a latte and a Danish, then joined Basima at the table. "Did you send me a message?" Sarah asked.

"Maybe."

Sarah dug around in her purse and found the heart. "Was it this?"

Basima had been at her house on New Year's Eve. They always celebrated together by watching old movies and toasting with Martinelli's cider at midnight. Basima knew her way around Sarah's kitchenette. She could have put the heart in the cereal then.

Basima smiled at her. "How long have we been friends?"

"Since we were six," Sarah said. They had met in kindergarten, and gone through grade school, middle school, and high school together. They had gone to college together to get their degrees in library science. They had roomed together all four years of the undergraduate program, and then Basima had gone for her Master's, while Sarah went to work.

"Have you ever felt a spark between us?" asked Basima.

"What?" Sarah said. She had had crushes on boys all her life, and never acted on them. She lifted a finger and held it out to Basima, who lifted her own index finger and reached toward Sarah. She stopped half an inch from Sarah's finger, and Sarah brought her finger closer. A spark jumped between them. "Whoa!"

"I got tired of waiting for you to figure it out," Basima said, and then blushed and stared at the table top.

Sarah bit her lip. Here was Basima, her best friend, finally letting her know something new to Sarah. Sarah, who could talk to cockroaches, but was often tongue-tied when it came to people. Things would be so much easier if Basima was an alien.

"Do you have a decoder ring?" Sarah asked.

Basima blinked, then looked up at her, wide-eyed. "As a matter of fact," she said, reaching into her giant orange purse, "I do."

"Wanna come home and meet my alien cockroach?" asked Sarah.

QUEEN OF PENTACLES

Holy Viper of the Old Greek Diner

~ Marilee Dahlman

Stupid and nasty, his enemies called him. Nico tried to ignore the sting of such insults. After all, at the crumbling Demeter Diner in downtown Chicago, who was in charge? Him. The remarkable Nico, newly elected leader of a great society. The beauty of it! Dark serpents hissing and snapping as they writhe over peeling linoleum, twisting through the rhythms of daily life, cycles of hunt and sleep, attack and dormancy. Violent creatures, but also civilized, still following ancient Greek traditions—gymnastics and track races, leisurely steam baths, and seasonal festivals honoring the goddess of rebirth, Demeter. She hadn't appeared in six thousand years and blight had ravaged the world for the last five hundred. On the diner's eastern wall, a fresco of the goddess stood faded but watchful. She wore black robes and held a basket of wilting poppies, the bright red a symbol of resurrection, as all molting serpents well-knew.

Nico turned his attention away from the goddess and back to the assembly. He slid his tongue across his fangs and cleared his throat. Ah, democracy. It was a splendid thing. "We must restore the values of past generations," he said, emphasizing every s with a long hiss. He'd assumed his favorite perch atop the host stand. The assembly packed the diner's floor, broad heads arched high and tails vibrating.

Zander, his old nemesis, reclined on the cracked table of the corner booth. Gray-scaled and well-oiled members of the old guard surrounded him, all comfortable on the plush leather seats. Zander slowly coiled and uncoiled his long, heavy body, waiting for silence. Nico's venom glands contracted. These old males with their soft bellies and milky pupils. They lived in luxury, nothing but fancy degrees and lineage justifying their power. And Nico remembered well his first day serving in assembly when Zander had called him a "small-snouted distraction," and the rest of the old guard snickered.

Today, they wouldn't laugh.

Zander raised his head to speak. "We are overcrowded. Food is scarce and you—"

"Treasonous elites!" Nico's hissed mutter provoked the thud of tails against the floor. Wind shook the diner's roof. The day darkened and earth groaned with another eruption of the new volcano on Lake Shore Drive. "Rumors of apocalypse are greatly exaggerated," Nico went on. "I will tell you the true threat! Do you know what it is? Barbarians! They approach from all sides! The solution?"

The assembly began chanting. They all knew the answer.

"Gates!" Nico roared. "We shall build gates of gold. Beautiful gates. Gates like you've never seen before."

Maria, his chief ally and serpent-in-charge of stores, met his gaze. Red scales circled her throat like a ruby necklace. Colonels stood at attention, medals from the wolf-war gleaming. The assembly screamed chants. Nico nodded, and Maria and the colonels slithered toward Zander. The ruling old guard unceremoniously slunk away, leaving Zander alone to face the mob. Over his forked tongue, even at this distance, Nico could smell the old snake's fear.

"Gates won't stop the permanent setting of the sun." Zander's words were soft. Maria and the colonels, trailed by the assembly, crawled closer. The chanting stopped.

"This elite has failed us. Now—prove your heroic virtues!" Nico's final word ended in a screaming hiss.

The assembly followed his order. Fresh meat was indeed scarce these days, but that night they feasted well on Zander-fleshed gyros.

The next few months unraveled in glorious fashion. The weather worsened but that was nothing new. With Zander finished, Nico wielded extraordinary power, aided by allies who believed in strength above all else. The old diner seethed, a boiling pit of carnivorous back-biting and treachery among his own supporters and subversion by Zander loyalists and gray-scaled philosophers. But Nico reigned popular. He dispatched soldiers to canvas the city, find prey and fetch it back to the diner, usually mice or rats and once a small deer. He ordered it hung

bloody on stakes and organized savage wrestling compe-
titions awarding prey as the prize. Citizens needed en-
tertainment to fill the dim days of existence, and the violence helped solve the chronic over-population issues.

"The solution is to be tough," Nico raged triumphantly
from his pedestal. As a young serpent, he'd been a strong
contender in track contests and once placed first in the
all-age high-jump. As an adult, he couldn't count the
number of times he'd smashed the head of an adversary,
sunk his fangs deep into prey, and ingested still-throb-
bing red flesh all for himself. Others could get tough, or
they could eat worms.

Then, one day, he lost.

A young soldier named Albert was toying with a wig-
gling lizard just outside the diner's kitchen. Nico smelled
the morsel and his head darted toward it, saliva already
filling his mouth. Albert, instinctively and quite stupidly,
whipped his tail and struck Nico with a stunning blow.
"*Waste* him," Nico hissed, head swimming. A colonel
promptly complied, and seconds later Albert's body was
being dragged to the kitchen. Nico trailed after and began to consume Albert whole.

The next day, another warning sign.

Nico lay on the kitchen tile, blood cool, mind drifting,
still digesting large hunks of Albert. Reeling from his
loss, his head and ego bruised, Nico had gorged and re-
treated to the crawlspace under the ovens for a long day
of digestion. He didn't especially love the diner's kitchen,
and rarely hung out there, a windowless place of utter

darkness. He preferred to lounge on the cold asphalt of the cracked parking lot and gaze up at the stars, wonder what it would be like to fly, serve as a winged serpent pulling Demeter's chariot, starlight reflecting from his orange-flecked scales for all to see.

His numb mind barely registered Maria's voice. It oozed low, somewhere near the back pantry with its empty bottles of olive oil and crackling parchment paper.

"He's *lost* it."

Nico tensed. He swallowed and forced down a juicy burp.

Voices murmured low.

Maria's voice again: "He says he saw ghosts."

Nico's jaw tightened. He'd mentioned that in confidence during an ouzo-drenched evening last week. He had simply mentioned that now and then, in his moments of glory on the host stand, he'd experienced some spiritual moments. Flashes, of a sort. He had witnessed ghosts of humans at the tables, servers striding down the aisles with moussaka, the aroma of spiced lamb filling the air. Ephemeral traces of the past, perhaps. Or maybe—in this world of endless molt and rebirth, existence at the mercy of the goddess of food and famine—some hint of the future.

"The assembly will support me." Maria's voice again. Not argumentative. *Authoritative.* The conniving reptile!

Snatches of words: *Poison. Slice. Smother.*

Albert's clogging remains sent darts of heartburn up Nico's throat. Smothering. Of all the ways to die, it would be the worst. The ignominy of it. To die smashed to the ground, night sky hidden by crawling, angry bodies above him. A plot! His own allies! The rest of the night he couldn't sleep. He stayed alert, frozen in his hiding place, listening to the plotters crunch and suck on the rest of Albert's remains. By morning, Nico had a plan.

He summoned the assembly.

In the main corridor unfurling from the entrance, booths to one side and counter on the other, the serpentine governing class spread before him: traitorous Maria, hard-scaled colonels, stretching and sanguine athletes, smirking poets and philosophers, a few silent and glaring Zander loyalists in the cheap seats near the back patio, and—his real source of power—all the rank-and-file who represented the common snake. True believers, who understood that viper society needed to be strong and secure, above all else.

From atop the host stand, Nico reared back and bellowed. "The golden gates—"

Gates, gates, gates! The answering chant erupted before he could finish. The enthusiasm! Back-stabbing Maria, the smug colonels—he'd show them. He eyed the philosophers, wondered what sort of false and twisted stories they would spin about him next. There was Bertrand, black-tailed and weathered, Cinder with a red triangular scale below his eye like a bloody teardrop. Devious creatures, these philosophers and their writings. At least they had the sense to wince and cower, silver-edged backs pressed against the Demeter fresco.

The chanting finally quieted enough for Nico to speak again.

"I have an important announcement." He paused for effect. "I shall embark on an odyssey."

Heads cocked all over the restaurant. His words weren't part of the usual script.

"A brief journey, but important."

He caught Maria's gaze. Her vertical pupils darkened and painted red lips twitched.

"I shall find the strategically correct location to construct the first gate. A shining golden gate, which shall strike fear and wonder in the hearts of all. I shall mark that place with my commanding scent, and loyal workers will begin to build." Nico drew a long breath. "And I shall brave the primitive barbarians to do it!"

Nico bared his fangs. The crowd screamed and drummed tails in support of their leader.

Nico set forth on his odyssey after an appropriate amount of scale-to-scale tail contact and speeches. He selected several bodyguards and a poet to accompany him, all of them young and hungry. The poet Pieter would compose an epic and recite it upon their return. This would add incomparably to Nico's overall mystique. Maria and the colonels would stay at the diner. In his absence, they could take the heat for limited fresh food. Nico departed in glory, with chants and applause following in his wake long after the diner fell out of sight.

"We'll return with fresh kills, while we're at it," Nico said. "A promotion to captain to whoever spots a deer!" The three young guards flicked their tails in pleasure. They fanned out in protection formation.

"May Demeter protect the *lives* of this brave *five*," said Pieter.

Nico grunted. Not the best poet, but it was impossible to find a decent poet or philosopher who wasn't a secret Zander loyalist. Why didn't the elites understand that the gates were a symbol? Golden gates represented superiority, virtue, the prowess of their society compared to all others.

They slithered through a city smashed by wind and earthquake. Caved in, crumbling buildings, streets steepled by tectonic grinds, glass everywhere. Nico didn't mind the journey. The cool air, days short and dim, the stars always shining. Snakes hadn't caused this destruction. It was the humans, of course, and they hadn't been spotted in years. Deadly carnivorous cousins, but unlike serpents, humans were not gifted with the ability to regenerate.

"You'd better write something good," Nico said to Pieter. "I want a glorious vibe. Lots of action."

Pieter would have to get creative. They'd encountered nothing living yet, aside from a few insects, and who cared about those? The desolation disturbed Nico but didn't surprise him. He'd been a young serpent once, out scrounging for all he could find. Life was supposed to be a cycle, but the whole world seemed in permanent decline. All the more reason to grab what power he could, however he could. His mind wandered to next steps, once he'd deposed of Maria and a few colonels and squeezed the entire ruling class into gasping prey under his complete control.

When he returned to the diner, he would phase in new rites of violence. That's why their serpentine eco-system was so successful. Resources were limited, and would only become more so. Fierce competition—fangs snapping, tails lashing, beautiful snake-on-snake blood games—they weeded the population down to size. Survival of the fittest. And, at the moment, he—Nico—was fittest of all. Maybe they could wage another pointless war against wolves. He'd carve society down so that the best cuts of meat went straight to him on a silver platter.

Their little band kept slithering.

"Ah, darkness upon darkness . . ." said Pieter. "Has our wrathful goddess provided grain for these creatures?"

Nico twisted his upper body to look up. There—perched on the roof of church—a thousand crows watched their progress. Some flapped wings and paced, others sat still as rain-battered gargoyles. Ugly creatures, but under the feathers beat blood and warm flesh. A thousand meals, tantalizingly within sight and out of striking distance. Nico's belly grumbled. Oh, but to have a god's strength! His cursed form bound always to earth. He had only his cruel wits and fangs to serve his needs.

"We are growing near," Nico said. He could sense the impatience and fatigue of the young guards. The poet trailed behind, always short-of-breath. "All of this territory belongs to us, conquered long ago by our heroic ancestors who came from the old world, Greece." It was true. They all knew it. "It is up to us to secure it for future generations."

Even Nico felt tired now. It was far enough. They should stop here, near this human church. One of the guards claimed he spotted pigs to the east, another said he'd spotted a patch of living cornstalks. Red-tinged vapors oozed up from cracks in the earth, providing a dramatic effect. Nico clicked his tongue against his fangs, considering. It didn't matter what site he selected for the first golden gate. They did not actually have any gold, for one thing. But still, Nico's body kept contracting and stretching, skirting over gravel, every instinct demanding that he keep going.

Soon those instincts proved correct. He sensed something in the distance. They all heard it: a relentless roaring. Like thunder, but softer, more controlled, shouts of a crowd at the last moment of a hundred-yard dash. But if these were united voices, they didn't stop.

"Danger ahead," Nico hissed. "Barbarians."

It could not be actual barbarians. There weren't any. A few prowling coyotes, perhaps, or unauthorized frog colonies squatting in concrete lagoons.

"Work it in," said Nico, with a look back towards Pieter, who'd fallen out-of-sight behind broken rubble. "The sound."

"Yes, composing in my mind," gasped Pieter. "I have lyrics, meter, meaning. Ah—"

A scream from the poet, suddenly cut off. Nico and the guards stopped and stared at each other.

Maria? The colonels? "Close in," Nico ordered.

They did, but too late. As they slithered toward Pieter, tall and hairy creatures grasping spears lunged toward them. Not monkeys, not gods . . .

"Humans," said a guard in a low whisper.

Nico barely heard it. For he was already escaping, every muscle flexing, his head, belly and tail grasping for traction on earth and propelling himself forward, every survival instinct in his body raging—find darkness! Now! Metal clanged on stone inches from his head. Pain burst along his spine before he managed to reach safety of a narrow pipe. The steel compressed his bleeding body, but he was safe for the moment. He winced at the hissing cries and moans behind him.

He slithered on. When the pipe ended, he chose routes offering the most darkness, always moving closer to that roaring sound. It was unfortunate about the others but he'd eventually work his way back to the diner. Lone survivor—he could build a true hero persona. And humans returned! The assembly would feed on that news for a long time.

A strong fishy smell mixed with mud-slick metal slid over Nico's tongue. Without warning, he came upon it, and he drew up short. An ocean lay before him—a place that, he was certain, had once been part of the city. Now, it was towering cliffs battered by swirling black waters, buildings and streets perched along a precipice. Howling winds and smashing earthquakes would send more concrete and glass sliding to a watery burial. To the north, a river spewed water into the ocean, creating a misty, deafening waterfall.

This was a gate. Towering cliffs and endless dark waters. A divine, living gate. Nico sighed—even if they could build golden gates, it would pale in comparison to this. He lifted his gaze to the stars and the lone moon struggling to control the waves. Huge black birds with scaled wings spun in lazy circles above the water. Nico dropped his head to the mud and shut his eyes. How he envied them, the ability to soar, their commanding gaze for miles!

He sensed a close and familiar scent. He whipped around, poised to strike. Serpents surrounded him in a half-circle, cornering him with the cliff to his back.

"Your reign is over, Nico."

Nico stared in dismay. It wasn't Maria or the colonels. The scales of these snakes were weathered, their dark eyes cloudy from years of squinting at texts. Black-tailed Bertrand, Cinder with the bloody teardrop, and three of their weak-spined philosopher pals.

"Elites." Nico snapped his tail and glared. "Zander loyalists! Lying and lazy philosophers! Molt your weak scales and reveal the traitor beneath!" Words that the supporters liked to hear. But these five philosophers just nodded as if expecting the tirade.

The wind strengthened. Nico hugged his body close to the ground and raised his head. "This is assassination." He kept his tone firm and grave.

They answered him with a sharp, unified hiss. Nico backed closer to the cliff's edge.

"I'll enjoy watching you plunge to your death," Bertrand said. "A fatal end to your power-hungry rule. You shall fall!"

Fall, fall, fall, they chanted.

Fear chilled Nico's cold heart to ice. This was indeed a bad way to perish. A long slide into oblivion, drowning by water and pure darkness. Could he fight? His stomach turned. These were creakingly old snakes but he was outnumbered, exhausted from the journey, and his spear wounds still seeped blood. He looked again at the stars. Perhaps there would be an odyssey beyond this one, another life, privilege and power beyond anything he had experienced on lowly earth. He shivered, feeling his scales harden. By the goddess, he was molting from fear.

He hissed with all his strength. "Oh lady of the great cycle of life and death, my queen Demeter—"

The assassins writhed closer, eyes wide, eager for the kill. "You use the name of the holy mother in vain! Across your deceitful lips and putrid fangs!"

Nico spat. Venom harmless without a bite, but the splatter across Bertrand's face felt gratifying. He had the right to invoke the divine. "Goddess of famine—"

"Goddess of *fertility*!"

Nico could scream louder. "Goddess of hunger—*vengeance—RAGE!*"

The assassins replied in joined scream that drowned the roar of wind and waves. "The law-bringer! Our lady of civilized existence!"

"Matron of decay," Nico muttered. He hunched his spine and prepared for stinging blows that would send him hurling over the edge. He breathed in, sensing the reptile scent of his assassins, the fishy waters below . . . and the sweet aroma of poppies in bloom. Nico frowned.

The serpents crawled closer. "Fall, fall—"

The chant was cut off with a collective gasp. The snakes froze, their unblinking eyes targeting something behind Nico. Near his tail, he sensed heat. A beautiful heat of melting gold, the dark heat of a heart burned black over fire. His inner ear vibrated with the sound of a scrape of stone and wretched moan.

He slowly turned.

A female in human form, dripping and wild, wrenched herself over the cliff's edge to safe ground. With dignified speed, she hauled herself upright. Clouds freed the moon to cast its light upon the woman. She wore a rotting black gown and cloak. Her hair hung in thick braids, her skin gleamed as if swept with oil, and the veins in her wrists and hands were dark, like snakes squirmed within her flesh instead of blood. She wielded a goat's horn spilling plump seeds.

Nico stared, cool air sliding over his fangs as he gasped for breath. All this time, living even deeper than he, in some dark cave beneath a cliff, above a sea?

"Demeter," the other snakes murmured, bowing low.

She ignored them and flung seeds that arched high. Nico followed their flight and saw that humans had advanced close to attack again. Now they cowered. The seeds sprung to life as living plants and an instant later dropped their fruit and grains. The humans shrieked with pleasure and gathered them.

Demeter raised her hands to the stars and clapped them in summons. At this, Nico screamed in delight. Streaking down from the heavens was a golden chariot pulled by a team of glowing, winged serpents.

"Take me, take me, take me!" Nico and the elites screamed. This was their queen. She brought destruction—ashes, rising water, darkness. But also, growth and life. The grand cycle. Nico imagined wings sprouting from his scales. He could see it—feel it—gliding through the night sky with the deity on divine missions. "Take me," he whispered. "I will serve you. I will serve you *best.*"

Demeter heard him, she heard them all, the hissing cries of the serpents desperate for attention. Fear ravaged Nico's soul—not of her, not of death, but of being ignored, forgotten, forced to accept the same fate as the lowly others. Demeter gazed down, her braids curling as if each was alive, her flesh glowing. Nico coiled his body, and with all his might, he sprung toward her, the longest, highest jump his body had ever achieved.

Demeter caught Nico and held him like she wanted to hold him. She raised him, far higher above the ground than he'd ever been before.

At her warm touch, Nico shuddered with a vision. An all-consuming sense of his future death and rebirth. Not wings. His cold blood would someday become warm ash. The ash would become sprout and stalk and bloom handsome scarlet, that striking color, that symbol of death and resurrection.

And then it was over.

Demeter gently placed him back into the mud and stepped onto her chariot. The gold flashed as she rose higher and disappeared. The only sign of where she'd gone was the eastern sky, where, for the first time in many years, a sunrise radiated bright yellow.

Nico set off for the diner, the sun warm on his back. The goddess's touch had healed his wounds, and he soon crawled out of his old skin. His new scales, a whole new self, shone bright and black. Nico and the philosophers were quiet on the return journey, reflecting. Tears crept down Nico's face, but he also found that his raw feelings soon faded and the practicalities of life reasserted themselves. Glares from the philosophers disturbed him and he moved quickly, staying out of reach of any strike.

They reached the diner during quiet twilight, snakes waking from afternoon naps on quake-battered asphalt, stretching in preparation for nocturnal hunts. "Nico!" the snakes cried. "Sunlight! New life!"

Indeed, Nico could see green weeds stabbing through concrete cracks, clover reaching over the rim of pots that stood sentry at the diner door. Inside, taking up his speaking position atop the host stand, he spied new spider in a corner and a beetle scurrying across the linoleum.

"The gates?" the assembly inquired. "Barbarians?"

"Forget the gates!" Nico hissed. "And never mind the barbarians." The philosophers slithered in and took up seats near the back patio. Maria and the colonels sat close by. Nico's mind squeezed and churned. His gaze lifted to the faded fresco of the goddess. In front of everyone, more scales shriveled off his body and he heaved with silent tears. The assembly fell silent. Nico gathered himself enough to choke out words.

"We have been chosen. *You* have been chosen." Hundreds of snakes stared back at him. "Our whole community will be remade. We are all woven together, loyal to the divine lady of the cycle of life and death." Nico eyed the philosophers, who slowly nodded agreement. "Our fate is clear. We shall rebuild her altar, and renew the ancient practices of worship. We thank her, she who has given us dry scales, cool blood, the ability to regenerate, to remake ourselves and our lives." Nico paused and cried out: "Oh goddess of fertility and famine, I am your lowly servant, the viper. Hear my hissing prayer for a freshly reborn regime! A *righteous* regime!"

Assembly tails began to pound. He counted quickly. Close to three hundred snakes. Far too many, even if the new light on earth brought many mice and rats. He composed his face to a stern expression and stared down the assembly. "Those who don't shed their old skins and comply with the ideals of the new order will meet the consequences. They shall—"

"Burn!" a philosopher shouted from the back.

Burn, burn, burn, the assembly chanted. The heads of the assembly bobbed up and down. Even Maria and the colonels followed suit. Someone lit incense.

"As your leader," Nico said, "I shall decide who must burn!"

The assembly roared its assent and continued its chant.

Nico demanded garments reflecting his elevated spiritual status, and young snakes quickly fetched him a veiled headdress and beaded vestments, crafted in some past generation that had first settled the diner. They found icons of the goddess and set up the chipped vases and plates and dusty paintings at the wall fresco to create an impressive altar.

Appropriately adorned, Nico kept hissing, fueling the crowd into religious fervor, enjoying his dominance, his brain growing dizzy with power and the sweet scent of myrrh. Night fell. He could no longer see the twisting and snapping assembly. But Nico was the most cold-blooded snake of all, and as the citizens of Demeter Diner writhed in righteous excitement, he could feel their heat.

Postcards From the Empty Nest

~ Rhonda Eikamp

Dear Bryn,

Sorry. I know you set up the smartphone & e-mail for me, honey, but I came across these unused postcards while cleaning out after the funeral—face it, your mother will never be digitized—& I felt the urge to put down in ink what's been happening here, everything about finding the Nest. I should start at the beginning. My, not much room on these things. I was so down after the funeral & you seemed in a hurry to fly out, I didn't get to talk to you like I wanted. Your father was a difficult man (an understatement, haha), you know that, but very responsible, & it's still hitting me how many things he took care of that are my responsibility now. Just thing things. Taxes, washing the car. You'll know when you get old—there's an energy seeps out of the mind & it can't turn itself to things. It was about a week in that I forgot to close the garage door for the night. He'd been the one to do that, see. I woke up in the morning knowing, rushed out. Nothing stolen. The car was there. Hit the button to close the door, watched it go down & that's when I discovered the silver circle. Big as a platter, there on the garage ceiling. The door had hidden it. Like a trick of the dawn light, or my dreams still percolating in me. I knew it hadn't been there the day before. I go to stand under it & I can see it's strands, rustling a little with the air. There's a cloth we used to call peau-de-soie, satiny but hefty, always in colors of metal or transparent jewels. The wedding-dress sheen. It rippled like that (or rather it stopped when I stood under it). But such a perfect circle, like bread mold. Like silver-white hair growing out from the center. I should have done something about it then, but it was just another thing, & I didn't want to deal with things. The problem is, every morning it's been a little bigger. I know you were always afraid of spider eggs & I just wanted to warn you—in case by chance you're back soon for a visit & I forget—don't go in the garage. (So—that gets that out of my system some. Really not much room on these things!)

—Love, Mom

☉

Dear Bryn honey,

Hope you get these in the right order.

You know when you see a face in an object & then you can't stop seeing it? (You may have a face like that in your life someday.) This is after it started to bulge in places. Grew about as big around as the roof of the car, though off to the side, in the empty space. I've started walking round & round every day gazing up, studying details of it, tighter & tighter circles until sometimes I'm spinning in place with my head thrown back. Makes me dizzy. (You used to do that as a child, arms stretched to the blue sky. Do you remember?) Don't worry what the neighbors think, the Nest is only visible with the garage door closed, remember. When the light from the little window hits it right (but it casts its own light), a face appears. Very plain, no particular features. A nonface, an unface, no one I know. I stopped thinking Nest so much & started thinking Face, telling myself, You've got to do something about the Face. But I never got around to it. Today, though, spinning slow like that underneath it, squinting hard, I caught sight of a kind of crack or rip in it, a darker hairline in the silver. Like a flap. Looked to be wavering with the motion of air, or maybe squirming, & I started thinking of all the things that could come out of a nest like that.

Your father would always get rid of the wasps' nests around the house. He'd slosh gasoline on them to stun them before he knocked the nest down. I know you think your mother's not tough, an old homebody (I'd have gone to work when you were older if your father hadn't been so touchy about being the breadwinner), but here I was today, up on the trunk of the car with a broom & a gas can. Figured I could just about reach it from there. Felt a little wavery myself. You were probably too young to remember that scandal with old Lily Carston down the street, lived alone, how they found her bruised with a broken wrist on her bedroom floor after she signalled that bracelet alarm, naked from the waist down? Swore she couldn't remember a thing & they figured the worst, till she confessed she'd fallen off her dresser after she climbed up to look at her hemorrhoids in the mirror. I felt like that (not about the haemorrhoids, honey) but thinking: if I fall this'll be hard to explain. Found in a pool of gas with a broken hip (or not found at all). Wasn't sure how I was going to slosh up there with that can. But when I straightened up I hesitated. Up close the Nest was so beautiful. The weave of it so structured, ridged. It wasn't a Face up that close, there were whole cities in there, a million tiny buildings, & me a god gazing down—up—onto it from its sky. And that's when the Nest

☉

B.,

Sorry. Ran out of room on the last card. That's when it spoke. It said, Water fountains.

That flap, turns out, is a mouth, though the sound (sounds by now) does not come from there but rather from all over it—a thrum, piano wire, church organs. Chords you feel deep down. A bone sound. I'll admit I said, Henry? (Silly, I know. Years of marriage will do that to you.) I was down on the floor by then, half-fell off the car & hurt my ankle, crawled into the corner & just sat with my knees pulled up, staring. After a long time it said, Brainstorming. I could hear the disgust in the voice then (the non-voice, unvoice), & it made sense. You surely recall how your father hated drinking fountains. Unpredictable intelligence, he'd claim—one high & spraying, the next one low & seepy, icy or tepid (he loved that word), germ colonies of the masses & you'd cry when he wouldn't let you use them. But you probably didn't know brainstorming was one of his hates too, how he'd come home from those mandatory meetings ranting how younger men could steal his ideas because it all came out of the session, created by the one mind working together & where was the credit where credit was due. I hunched there in the garage corner, thrummed through by that sound, & it made sense, that if there was anything of him to survive it would be the hates. (Wouldn't it?) Because in life they had been so large. I felt light, empty, always air anyway & now even that pumped out of me, just an old church filled with the organ sound of his gripes. I felt the Nest would float down onto me then, odd thought, almost wanted it to, but me & the Nest had both grown very still, not wavering anymore. Just waiting.

After a while it said, Country music.

☉

Bryn,

Got your message on the answering machine. You don't have to worry about me, hon. Impossible's what you make of it—if you're handed impossible lemons, make crazy lemonade.

I ditched the gas can the next day. Figured I could get up under it with the broom & loosen it, make it drop. Like turning a pancake. Didn't know what I'd do if I got it down on the garage floor. Look it over maybe close

up, take my own good time. Maybe touch it. The silver
threads seemed to have gotten thicker in just a day, not
hairs so much as gel, it rippled away from the loose edge
I poked, all those ridges & structures softening & swell-
ing, like it'd love to just shake me off, but I wasn't having
it. I was a god giving that city an earthquake. Just when
the broom was wedged up under it good, it moved away.
Fast. Scuttled all the way across the ceiling, toward the
door to the kitchen that I'd left open.

I almost fell again. Not because it was its own creature,
loose & moving (but still suckered to that ceiling). It was
the shock of how it moved. Because, honey, I recognized
that scuttle. There was that disgust in the way it hunched
away from me, if a blob can be said to hunch. Annoyed.
(Can't think of a better word). If the list of hates hadn't
made me certain of what I was looking at, that did. He
waited for a second at the door to see how I'd react, then
went on into the house, sort of flowed across the lintel
like an earthworm (a very large, very silver earthworm, an
earthworm city) & I followed. Found him spread across
most of the kitchen ceiling. It made him seem even larger,
being inside like that, so unexpected against my ivy-pat-
tern curtains & the plastic fruit on top of the fridge. So
organic (I suppose that's the word). A thing that belongs
outside brought inside. Out-of-place. Not dirt but something like it. A neck of him oozed out from the rest, still
attached, inched on across the top of the door into the
den, inspecting it for changes. The voice said, Cobwebs.
The sound of those hate words was larger too now it was

inside, it thrummed in the walls & the floor. I admit I don't clean the corners up near the ceilings like I should. Call waiting, it said, & then: Forgetfulness.

I felt all empty again hearing that. All my air gone. The whole house has been airless since that moment it said that, a box of airless. I think it's what's caused this latest growth spurt these past few days. Aren't there amoebas that grow in a lack of oxygen? He's so big now, honey, you wouldn't believe. The only ceiling in every room, worming through the top of every door. That voice goes on night & day with its rumbling list. Wicker headboards, horses rolling, funerals. The sound is like a storm that's passed but the thunder keeps reaching back for you. I dream it at night. Perfume, he said last night from the bedroom ceiling, just before I nodded off, & I said aloud into the dark: I know, it's why I never wore it. Your father hated fake scents, Bryn, liked the natural scent of me, he'd say. Never a romantic, but something about him saying that always made me feel happier.

I had good dreams that night.

Love for now. More later.

☉

Dearest Bryn,

Sorry I missed you again. I don't pick up much any-more. Please please don't jump on a plane, I know you have a busy life & it's not necessary. It's going too far though to say I'm imagining this, sweetie. No one could imagine something this big. I do have to stoop & that's an inconvenience. He's larger now than anything I've ever had in the house. Plus there have come to be certain (how do I say this delicately?) bulges, extending almost to the floor in every room, stalactites (or is it –mites?) that I have to detour around. Cottony columns, pillars, as if I was living in a soft silver temple. If I saw a Face before, I see something else in these Pillars. The tips bend toward me when I try to go around them. The words keep on rumbling of course, erupting from everywhere now, the whole house speaking when he does, a mumble so run together I hardly hear it anymore. Belt-buckles roses decaf tan-lines the squinting eyes lists. Hard to believe anyone could hate so many things. Meter-readers, snow in May, a letter with no return address. I'm tired of this on-and-on, Bryn, believe me, all his modern art's & his gnocchi's, all his hates rolled into that eternal mumble, but I sat there last week in the blue recliner as I often do these days, gazing up into that city that is more a huge heaving hill-country of silver grass, so close I can feel the thrum picking up my hair like static, & for a moment the mumble became words again.

Small dogs, sudden silences, tofu.

Child-proof caps? I suggested.

The quiet lasted too long. Wasn't there anything you loved, I asked. Even one thing.

Another silence. Then a word.

You.

Funny thing is, I'm not sure if he heard me or if he was

still listing. After a second the mumblings went on. Empty rooms, word games, a liar. I accept it for now, but I can't decide which he meant, Bryn, a hate or a love. I just can't. Can you?

What I think is that I have to stop thinking about it.

So you see you don't have to be afraid for me. The important thing is this—I could leave anytime if I wanted to, walk out the door & close it behind me, out to where there are no ceilings, & that is a thing he can't do. Because he is attached & I am not, see. I can tell myself he's been put in his place for once & it's enough for me. That no matter how much of the house he fills, with his mass & his staticky thrum that turns my head to liquid & his grasping Pillars—it's still an empty buzzing nest, whereas I'm filled with that energy I thought I'd lost. I may get a small dog. I may travel. I may. Even in my bent state (& it's very low now, since this morning I'm reduced to crawling) it would not be too hard. Those Pillars haven't blocked the doors yet entirely. I'll squeeze through to take this to the mailbox & then I'll come back in & think about it. What I mean to say, Bryn honey (running out of room again), is that you shouldn't be worried if you arrive & don't find me here because it will mean I've

KING of CUPS.

The Witches' Parliament

~ *Jordan Taylor*

"England is governed not by logic but by parliament."
~ Benjamin Disraeli

In a dark, secret wood stood a dark, secret house. The house was made of wood shingles and good English stone, with many rounded towers and cupolas and dull silver windows, and a wide, wrap-around porch on which no one would ever take lemonade. There was no garden, no drive, nor even a narrow path, its stone foundations rising from the dirt and the moss and the twisted roots as if it were a mushroom grown from the forest floor. On the peeling front door hung a knocker in the shape of an owl with dull citrine eyes, holding a twisted branch in its hooked beak.

The knotted trunks of oak and ash and thorn trees pressed close round the house on all sides, their branches overhanging the peaked eaves. No bit of sky showed its face in that wood. A chill wind rattled the branches and sent brown leaves dancing across the wide, bare porch. In England it was May. In the wood, it was whatever month the witches felt it should be.

A candle flared to life in the window of an upper story.

Owls swooped in and out of the house's rounded attic windows, circling the towers and perching on branches to await their turn to enter: small tawny owls and little gray owls with ruffled feathers, great horned owls with fierce hooked beaks, and even a few snowy owls with dark markings on their chests and wings, like the curling paper bark of a birch tree.

The owls disappeared into the dark, secret house in an endless stream, a great flock of owls, which is not called a flock at all, but a *parliament*.

In the downstairs of the house, a great many lights were lit all at once.

The inside of the house was full of light, now, and of witches, and owls. As each owl alighted on the upper landing of the grand, sweeping staircase it shivered into the form of witch—a woman young, or old, or somewhere in-between; beautiful, or ugly, or plain; fat or slim, dark or fair, sweet-tempered or passionate—so many women it seemed impossible that such a house, filled as it already was with patterned wallpaper and rich carpets and carved mantlepieces and over-stuffed furniture and candles and teacups and trinkets, could hold them all. Perhaps the house was larger inside than out, or perhaps the women-who-were-owls and the owls-who-were-women were actually very small, no bigger than the owls they'd been.

In any case, all were gathered in the front parlor now, talking over one another and shouting across their raised cups of tea. A fire crackled merrily in the hearth. A few younger witches shoved one another in a corner over who should get the last comfortable seat. The Lady Zenobia arched her white eyebrows and tapped her silver teaspoon against her bone china cup.

The room went quite as a grave.

"My sisters," the Lady Zenobia said, "You all know why our Parliament has gathered. We have been tracking this development for the better part of a year. I will open the debate." She paused to draw in a breath. "Should we interfere yet again?"

In most parliaments, speeches are punctuated by the warm and rousing call of "My brothers!" In the witches' parliament, one said "My sisters!" instead.

The Lady Zenobia raised her teacup to her lips as the room erupted into chaos around her. Though her long, thick hair was as white as bleached bone, her face was firm and unlined, her body beneath her rustling silk dress still that of a strong young woman.

"How dare he!"

"These *men*!"

"They think they can just take, and take, that their ambitions count for everything and ours for nothing—"

"After all our work! Wives made barren!"

"Princesses and uncles killed!"

"And one assassination diverted already!"

"She is *ours*!" a fierce witch proclaimed, and the cry was taken up round the room. "Ours, ours!"

"And so we will interfere on her behalf again," a decisive young witch spoke up. Her dark eyes flashed. "Or set our kind back another hundred years!"

"No more! This has gone far enough!" an old crone shrieked from the back. "We have broken our first rule! The first vow that we swore! *Do. Not. Interfere!*"

The Lady Zenobia cleared her throat.

The din subsided.

"'Do not interfere' is our *second* vow, Lady Anne," a round, middle-aged witch said tartly in the ensuing silence. "The first is 'Do no evil.'"

Lady Anne snorted and waved her hand in front of her face.

"We will take a vote, then," the Lady Zenobia said when the two had finished. "Those who would go back to the old ways, those who would watch, and wait?"

"And those opposed?"

"Then we will need to be closer than this." The Lady Zenobia waved her hand. "Green Park, I think."

In the depths of night, when even the theaters were closed, when the only traffic in London's streets were the most well-heeled gentlemen and ladies passing through on their way home from parties, and the most down-at-the-heels men and women passing through on their way to a penny-worth of coffee and bread from a stall before the workday began, Young England gathered in Simpson's cigar divan.

Simpson's was a typical lounge for wealthy gentlemen—a comfortable drawing room all of leather couches and polished wood and green-shaded gas lamps, above the cigar shop of the same name, on the Strand. Pop your head in on this night, and you'd be forgiven for thinking that Young England was a being made of cigar smoke and fog.

But there were three beings moving within that obscuring smoke, that secret fog, three beings in impeccable eveningwear with their hats set on their knees, cigars held languidly in their long fingers, cups of coffee on tables and trays. They had been through many cups of coffee, and their cigars had almost burnt down to stubs.

On a low, round table, in the center of the room, lay a brace of pistols, their barrels and stocks chased with silver scrolls. They shone wickedly in the light of the flickering fire in the hearth. None of the beings looked at them.

The pistols had been procured from a pawnbroker and moneylender in Covent Garden. This was meant to make them untraceable. None of the fashionable beings had thought to choose a more utilitarian pair.

"What England needs is a hero," the being with the mustache was saying. He stubbed his cigar out on the nearest tabletop, a horrid display of bad manners. "A King Arthur, to guide us through this Industrial mess, to lead and inspire the populace. Instead we're given a weak puppet, first of that philandering Whig," grunts heard round the room, "And then of a blasted German!"

"Yes," a dark being in the corner drawled from the depths of a leather armchair. His eyes flared from the midst of the cloud of cigar smoke which obscured his face. "Because the last Arthur we had did so well. After his disastrous run as Prime Minister, Lord Wellington is still cowering behind iron curtains in the depths of Apsley House." He slurped at his coffee with disgust.

"Peace, John, Dizzy," an elegant being with dark muttonchops spoke. "We are all in agreement here. Though I beg you, Dizzy, before you go any further, to remember the first attempt."

Had the beings not been gentlemen, they might have shuddered. The first man to attempt what they now spoke of had not only mysteriously failed, but been sent to Bedlam in perpetuity.

"Good god, George, must you bring that up again? The first attempt failed, so what?" the being called John blustered. "We are better men." He raised his eyebrows meaningfully.

Dizzy rolled his eyes as he puffed on his cigar. He was young, with the piercing eyes of a satirist. "I have told you both: I have seen the future that awaits England if we do not act. It is of this that I am afraid, not of our task. That I will gladly shoulder on my own, and leave the two of you out of it."

The other men waited as Dizzy took a small notebook out of his breast pocket to scribble the lines down: *I have seen the future . . . That I will gladly shoulder . . .*

"Seriously, Dizzy," George flung down his coffee cup in exasperation as the notebook and pencil were replaced, "No one knows what you mean when you speak like that—"

But John pounded his fist on the table, drowning George out. "Well said! If a man wants a thing done properly, then he must do it himself."

"I never heard you volunteer," Dizzy drawled, though his eyes were hard. He wrinkled his nose and gave a droll curl of his lip. "I suppose the action will necessitate some sort of uncouth *disguise*. I will have to visit Petticoat Lane tomorrow. What an *adventure*." He flicked a speck of ash from his trouser leg, rearranged the fabric so that the seam was a perfect straight line down his calf.

George gave him a stricken look. "I beg of you, for the last time, reconsider. Let John and I draw upon our fathers' funds, or use some of Mary Anne's—your debts are considerable, I know, but surely with her income you needn't do this yourself—"

"No," Dizzy's eyes flared. "I will not have her—or you—involved."

John folded his hands and said nothing.

"Think of your place in Parliament," George pleaded, the delicate lines of his face drawn tight. "You are the greatest influence we have. If caught, you will be arrested and tried. You will ruin your reputation, your ambitions, your dreams..."

Dizzy laughed, a quick bark of a sound. "My reputation is ruined already. And as for my dreams –"

"When you see the future," George tried, "Do you see no role for yourself?"

Dizzy rose from his chair, his face set. He stubbed out his cigar in a glass ashtray and flipped his silk hat onto his head before shrugging on his overcoat. He picked the pistols up from the table, testing their weight, and suddenly the two other beings could not look at him.

"*Ambition's debt must be paid*," he said, and he plunged the pistols deep into his overcoat pockets.

In the bright, secret house in the dark, secret wood, somewhere in Green Park, a witch turned over a card. She wore black velvet, tightly corseted, and a diamond brooch sparkled on her right shoulder. Curls of dark hair, touched with gray, spilled over the left. She was called Lady Grace.

Her lace cuffs trailed across the tarot spread, her long fingernails tapping the densely patterned backs of the cards. She sat at the head of the house's enormous dining table, the Lady Zenobia at her side. The other witches crowded around wherever they could fit, leaning into the heat of the candelabras which lined the polished tabletop. This was made easier by the fact that a small number of them were now missing.

"Seven of swords," Lady Grace said solemnly.

"Secrets," the witches all murmured. "Occult knowledge?"

"No, no," one scoffed. "It's the weapons in his pockets."

Lady Grace set the card aside with a flick of her wrist, and turned over the one which had been hidden behind it. The witches all gasped.

"Death."

Dizzy walked out of Simpson's and into the London night, his head still swimming with cigar smoke and dreams. Though it was early May, there was a damp chill to the air, and the fog clung to the cobbled streets. The air stank of factory smoke and sewage and the sea, even here.

He passed down the brightly-lit Strand and through vast, empty Trafalgar Square, his feet unconsciously directing him towards home and Mayfair.

His plan had been set for weeks; he'd only been waiting for John to procure the pistols and shot. Tomorrow afternoon, during her weekly Sunday drive along Pall-Mall in her open carriage, he would be waiting in the crowd, in disguise. As she passed him, he would step forward, and then—

He shook his head, dodging across the intersection with Haymarket Street. Then all he had foreseen would be averted.

It had been Dizzy's grandfather, for whom he was named, whom had introduced him to the Kabbalah. Though Dizzy's own father had baptized his entire family when Dizzy was twelve—had gone so far as to change their last name—his grandfather had wished to ensure that some wisdom, some traditions of their ancestors, survived.

Often Dizzy wished he had chosen someone else.

Unbidden came the image of his laughing Mary Anne: her chestnut curls, her pert mouth, her mirth-filled eyes.

But no, there was no reason for him to hesitate, none at all; his dreams had come to naught—his novels read by the masses but discounted by the critics and upper classes, his first speech to Parliament disastrous. Even Mary Anne—she well knew that his reasons in marrying her were mercenary. How, then, could she love him now?

The pistols in his pockets seemed to weigh more than they should, and he shuffled to a stop in the center of the street, his hands pressed to his eyes. Carriages and carts clattered around him. Drivers called out.

He would remain on the Back Bench his entire life, until he died, a creature of contempt.

"*Hath not a Jew eyes*?" he murmured to himself.

In the bright, secret house, the witches whispered amongst themselves, eyeing the overturned card.

"It is reversed," the Lady Zenobia said, unperturbed, and the fearful whispers changed to surprise.

"Rebirth?

Lady Grace turned over the next card, and this time the witches nodded. "There he is."

"The Hierophant. The high priest."

"Also reversed," one pointed out.

"Under different circumstances . . ." Lady Grace tapped the card.

"From what we have learned, he could be useful, no doubt," Lady Anne said.

In the witch's deck, the Hierophant was represented by a raven captured mid-flight, a rod held in his beak.

The young witch who'd been so set on their interference, who was called Lady Flora, reached out to touch the image on the card with one finger. "I've always wondered what the rod is meant to be," she laughed. "Lately it's looked almost like a nib pen!"

"*Shush*," Lady Anne said, and Lady Grace turned over the next card in her spread.

"The Queen of Wands." The witches exchanged knowing looks.

And, "The Two of Swords."

"Opposing forces."

"A clash between two great powers," the Lady Zenobia said.

Dizzy stood on the gently-lit path through Green Park, gulping breaths of the fresher cool air. He could not quite remember how he had gotten there—the park was not technically on his way home—though he did remember a wish to delay his homecoming, to clear his mind. A gentle breeze sent flower petals and leaves and scraps of rubbish dancing towards him.

His friends had spoken in terms of party affiliation, of puppets and leaders of men; while in his head churned the factories that splintered England's landscape and dined on the peasantry, the flies swarming the silent huts of India, the rooms of drugged sleepers in China.

And crouching at the center of England's destruction, like a dark, squat spider: the widow queen, her clinging web ensnaring the world.

He slipped his hands into his overcoat pockets, curled his fingers around the triggers of his pistols.

Soon he was stumbling in the darkness beneath the park's eaves, cursing the Select Committee for Urban Planning. Somewhere on the path behind him the widely-spaced gas lamps had run out, but he was no longer exactly sure where.

The path, too, had dwindled under his feet, to no more than a dirt foot-path. He could recall nowhere like this in Green Park.

A rush of air, past his left ear. He turned, drawing a gun and swinging it round. A glint of moonlight caught the silver-chased barrel, reflected from a pair of round, glowing eyes in the branches above him.

Coo hoooo.

Dizzy lowered his arm, his body trembling.

It was only an owl.

"The Nine of Swords," Lady Grace said. The light of the candelabras flickered over her still face.

"Dark dreams. Fear."

"The Two of Wands."

"He thinks he has made up his mind." The witches laughed.

"The Eight of Swords." Lady Grace smiled. "At last."

"He's entered our wood."

Dizzy crashed through piles of dead leaves, dodged around the ancient trunks of oak and ash and thorn trees, tripping over their twisted roots. The path through the dark wood—for Green Park this no longer was, could not be—had long since run out.

It should be May, he knew it was May, and yet the branches of the trees were all bare, a cold autumn wind shaking them. Owls swooped through the spaces between them, their eyes points of fire in the night, their calls climbing up his spine.

There was some magic at work here, the feeling of it set his teeth on edge—a magic that was not his.

An owl dived at him, knocking his hat from his head.

Panting, he ran on.

In the witches' House of Parliament, Lady Grace turned over the ninth card.

A Grecian woman, a blindfold around her eyes, held a pair of scales in one hand. Lady Grace's face lit with triumph. She reached for the final card in her spread.

"Shhh!" the Lady Zenobia hissed. "Did you hear that?"

The witches froze, Lady Grace's fingers hovering over the last unturned card.

Three loud raps, from the owl-shaped knocker on their house's front door.

The dining room was full of women.

After Dizzy's mad dash through the woods, it was brilliantly lit and suffocatingly hot, the walls papered in an absurdly feminine rose chintz. There were cards scattered across the vast tabletop, candelabras dripping wax, chairs crowded into every spare space. A needlepoint sampler hung on one wall.

"Pay Your Debts," it read, in an intricate gothic script.

Dizzy lingered in the doorway, his heart pounding under what seemed to be one hundred frank and unwavering gazes. He could feel his perfectly starched linen shirt sticking to his skin with sweat. The Lady Zenobia smiled at him as she swept through the maze of chairs to the head of the table.

It had been she whom had responded to his pounding fist on the front door. Three owls had swept into the impossible house behind him, carried on a gust of wind and a flurry of dead leaves. They'd alighted on the parquet floor, preening their ruffled feathers with tiny hooked beaks, while Dizzy struggled to catch his breath.

There had been acorns and insects and spiders' webs in his tousled hair and overcoat. Mud caked his buffed shoes and trouser cuffs. He looked up as the Lady Zenobia shut the door, running his hands through his hair and shaking out his clothes, and his grunt of disgust caught in his throat.

Where the three owls had been stood three young women, their hands folded demurely in front of their skirts.

"Welcome, Mr. D'Israeli," the Lady Zenobia said. She was dressed as a wealthy gentlewoman, and yet, as she turned towards him, her long hair swung loose behind her back like a child's.

Dizzy winced at the mispronunciation. "Disraeli," Dizzy had corrected her, "Please. Mr. Benjamin Disraeli, madam."

"I beg your pardon," he'd called as she led him from the hall, "But how do you know me? Why have you brought me here? And who—Where—" He'd faltered, and she'd paused before the set of glass doors which led to the dining room and turned back to him with a smile, the sort of smile a man could break himself on.

"We have been watching you, Mr. Benjamin Disraeli," she'd said. "We know all about you. Your family history, your deepest desires, your motives . . ."

Dizzy's breath hitched, and the two pistols pressed into his ribcage. "My motives?" he asked. And, in a hoarse gasp: "You work for Her Majesty?" His head spun with the implications.

The woman laughed at him, a deep sound like a funeral bell. "Of course not, Mr. Disraeli. We work for ourselves.

I am called the Lady Zenobia," she turned and shoved open the pair of glass doors, "And this is my Parliament."

It was then that he had frozen under the intent gaze of a hundred pairs of eyes.

Her voice, from behind him, was teasing. "We are witches, Mr. Disraeli."

The Lady Zenobia's seat at the head of the table was like a throne, higher than those around her, the back carved into three spiraling points.

As she sat, Dizzy's perception of the room shifted subtly to reflect a judge and jury, with himself standing in the place of the accused. He reached for his hat, found it gone, and stuffed his hands into his overcoat pockets.

"I hope I am not expected to make a speech," he quipped. "If this parliament has any concourse with mine, you'll know that I am hopeless in that regard." The room remained stonily silent, save for the collective breathing of one hundred or more women.

The Lady Zenobia arched her eyebrows. "Turn out your pockets, Mr. Disraeli."

Dizzy squared his shoulders, his dark eyes flashing defiantly. He laid the pair of pistols on the table, amongst the cards, where they gleamed smugly in the brilliant light. His skin went cold as he took note of the image of blind Justice, her scales held high in one hand. The women exchanged glances, murmuring and shifting in their seats.

"Benjamin Disraeli," the Lady Zenobia said, her eyes hard, "You stand accused of plotting to commit high treason to kill the queen, Alexandrina Victoria I, God save her. How do you plead?"

"You have not seen what I have seen!" Dizzy thundered, and his anguished face swept back and forth across the room. "Swaths of dead—here, round the world—the loss of England's very way of life!"

The Lady Zenobia's eyes glinted. "And for this you would commit murder? The murder of your queen?"

Dizzy paused. The fire swept from his eyes, so that he seemed to shrink before the women's faces. "No," he admitted, pressing his palms to his eyes. "From the moment I took up the pistols, I've known that I could not." He shook his bowed head. "The thought of it was driving me mad."

"A convenient end," the Lady Zenobia mused, "Saving England from its fate," and Dizzy looked up at her in surprise.

She shook her head. "You say that England's way of life will be lost." Her voice rose, and she spread her arms wide. "I say, let England lose it! The world of men is passing—let it pass!" The women surrounding her shouted out in agreement.

"You say that you can see the future," the witch who sat at the Lady Zenobia's side spoke up. "Have you seen this?" She leaned towards him, over the table, and a diamond flashed on her shoulder. "Two decades from now, when her husband dies, Victoria will mourn for the better part of a century, but she will never marry again. Do you understand? She will reign solo for the rest of her life!"

"The widow queen." Dizzy stared at her. "But she will plunge the world into darkness."

"In all darkness," the Lady Zenobia said, "Is a glimmer of light." She seemed to have grown taller, her eyes sharp and bright as jewels, her voice filling the room, and Dizzy took a surprised step back, hitting the cooler glass of the door.

A young witch with dark eyes stood up. "A decade from now, a woman will write that women have been excluded from every aspect of government but the highest, the regal, at which Victoria succeeds."

Women around the room murmured in agreement. "She is the starting point, the lynch-pin," their voices echoed. "You would take that away from us?"

Dizzy stretched his hands out to them. "If you have seen all this, then you must understand! The Kabbalah has shown me these things for a reason—a great war which will cover the world in yellow clouds of gas." The witches were shaking their heads, "Trenches that split the countryside like arteries of black blood." He stepped forward, trembling, willing them to understand. "And all because of her! I see it constantly, awake and in my dreams. If I am not strong enough to stop it, you must be!"

"And all because of her," the Lady Zenobia repeated thoughtfully. She shook her head, and Dizzy's heart sank. "We will not be silenced. We will not give her up. But she will make mistakes, yes. Bad decisions. War. Mankind will tear itself apart," her eyes glittered. "That is what mankind does."

"She will need to be balanced," the witch in the diamond brooch said.

"A Prime Minister from the opposing party, perhaps?" the young witch spoke up. "A man."

"Her opposite," another said, "Creative and empathetic, with a quick wit."

"Someone far-seeing." The Lady Zenobia smiled wryly.

"Someone to check her."

"As she will check him."

Dizzy clutched the edge of the tabletop, a howling wind sweeping through his mind. He must have missed something. Surely, they could not mean . . . Would such a solution even work?

The Lady Zenobia stood up from her place at the head of the table and came towards him. "We will not let you wriggle out of your destiny so easily, you see?" She held out her hand, and one of the younger girls put a branch of willow in her palm.

"You will leave the pistols here," she said, as she paused to stand before him. "If you agree to this, I must take the memories and the knowledge from you as well. And from your friends." She raised the willow wand, her long fingers loose. "The Kabbalah may show you other things, but it will never again show you this."

Dizzy looked into her eyes, a blue as cold and remote as the stars. He suddenly felt wrung out, exhausted, his horror and his anguish gone. Impossibly, hope was rising in his breast. This was what he had dreamt of, a dream kept secret from all, even Mary Anne.

No middle-class Jew had ever been made Prime Minister.

The Lady Zenobia smiled as if reading his thoughts. "It

will be no small task. But you will not shoulder it alone. We can promise you that." The witches nodded behind her.

"Yes," Dizzy said, and he bowed his head and knelt.

"*You will find friends in life,*" the Lady Zenobia spoke, and her voice once again filled the room as she tapped each of his shoulders with the willow wand. "*And they will be women.*"

Behind them, from her seat at the table, Lady Flora nudged the pair of pistols aside to surreptitiously turn over the final tarot card.

It was The Empress.

Dizzy stood in the middle of the Queen's Walk beneath the eaves of Green Park's rustling trees. The gas lamps shown around him, and overhead, the night sky was lightening to gray. He thrust his hands into his overcoat pockets against the chill in the wind, and for a moment he was surprised to find them empty.

He was sure he'd been carrying something—something heavy—but what?

He riffled through his other pockets, pulling out his notebook. He flipped to the latest page.

"It is not the task itself I fear, for I will not shoulder it alone," he read.

Where had he heard that? He shrugged and replaced the notebook.

There was no hat on his head. He must have misplaced it somewhere in the course of the night, but where?

Where had he been?

The only thing he could remember was a brass door-knocker, shaped like an owl, a willow branch held in its beak. Which of his friends' houses could that be?

He shook his head in confusion. He must have been very, very drunk.

He pushed his hands deeper into his pockets and set out for Mayfair, whistling one of his favorite drinking songs. Perhaps it was not too early to come across a flow-er seller in the streets. Mary Anne would be waiting for him, and she would be worried.

KNIGHT of SWORDS .

New Caldwell Metropolitan Guard Cold Case Files
On the Disappearance of Oliver Wolsey

~ John Klima

Item List

- *Hand-copied pages from Constable Marcus Gurney's journal*
- *Transcriptions of interviews conducted by Metropolitan Guard with various individuals:*
    - *Graham Douglas*
    - *Edgar Shipman*
    - *Roger Blokeman*
    - *[REDACTED]*
    - *Ignatius Howlett*
- *Meeting minutes from New Caldwell Tarot and Magic Guilds wherein discussion of Oliver Wolsey occurred:*
    - *Redhands (Health and Medicine Tarot Guild)*
    - *Speakers for the Decayed (Communication with the Dead Tarot Guild)*
- *Partial tarot deck of mixed provenance*
- *Longshoreman's hook, bloody (stored in paper as per instruction from the Blood Mage branch of the Metropolitan Guard)*

Health and Medicine Tarot Guild Meeting
Monday, August 3ʳᵈ, 1874

Members in Attendance
[REDACTED] Chair
[REDACTED] Vice-Chair
[REDACTED] Secretary
[REDACTED] Treasurer
[REDACTED] Chair-Elect
[REDACTED] Past Chair
[REDACTED] Director
[REDACTED] Director
[REDACTED] Director
Members Not in Attendance
[REDACTED] Director
[REDACTED] Director
[REDACTED] Director
[REDACTED] Director
Guests in Attendance
Oliver Wolsey
Staff in Attendance
Nym Vernon
Reynaldo Stafford
Edgar Cromwell

1.   Call to Order
Chair called meeting to order at six o'clock in the evening
of the third of August, 1874.

2.   Approval of Agenda

ON A MOTION MADE by **[REDACTED]**, SECOND-
ED by **[REDACTED]** and CARRIED, the agenda was
approved as circulated.

3.   Conflict of Interest

Director **[REDACTED]** recuses himself from discussion
of NEW BUSINESS due to a CONFLICT OF INTEREST.

4.   Approval of Previous Minutes

ON A MOTION DULY MADE by **[REDACTED]**SEC-
ONDED by **[REDACTED]** and CARRIED the draft
minutes of the Guild's meeting of the second of July were
approved as presented.

5.   Old Business
a.   Redhands Name

[REDACTED] opened discussion on the colloquial name
of the Guild—'Redhands'—which he disdains. **[REDACT-
ED]** asked the attending board for ideas of how to stop the
pernicious name from the public's tongues.

[REDACTED] stated that there was no way to control
the public and since 'Redhands' was spoken often under
auspices of fear, that the Guild should embrace it.

Followed a moment of shouting by several Guild
members including **[REDACTED]**, **[REDACTED]**, and
[REDACTED] among others. Chair banged the gavel
until the shouting wore down. He declared this business
closed.

Chair noted this was the sixteenth consecutive meeting that [REDACTED] had brought this item to the agenda with no solution and no movement towards change. It was declared to be un-agendable in the future.

b.   Membership

[REDACTED] reported that after reviewing membership files after last meeting there was no need to seek out new members. [REDACTED] apologized for wasting Oliver Wolsey's time as his petition for membership would not be brought to the Guild at this time.

6.   New Business

a.   Printing Press

[REDACTED] MADE A MOTION to stop using The Elementary Pot printing house and purchase a printing press for the Guild to create tarot cards in private. The MOTION was SECONDED by [REDACTED] and CARRIED via ROLL CALL VOTE.

b.   Card Manufacture

[REDACTED] made a subsequent MOTION that [REDACTED], while recused from discussion, be put in charge of purchasing the printing press and then card manufacture given his experience in the field. SECONDED by [REDACTED] and CARRIED via ROLL CALL VOTE.

7.   Committee Reports

None

8.   Staff Reports

Nym Vernon reported that the staff had found a solution for the rat problem in the Guild's kitchens, namely obtaining several cats. Vernon also reported that construction had finished on the upstairs residences and after a coat of paint the Guild officers could move in.

Edgar Cromwell reported that their current launderer had switched soaps and was causing their robes to become pink rather than retaining their deep scarlet. The Chair gave permission to seek a new launderer.

9.   Adjournment

ON A MOTION MADE by [**REDACTED**], SECONDED by [**REDACTED**] and CARRIED, the meeting was adjourned at nine o'clock.

﹥๏

Hand-copied transcript of Constable Marcus Gurney's journal, entry dated August 6th

Thinking back on last night I will endeavor to put my thoughts into a reasonable facsimile of sense and order.

Not long into my beat around the Nine Points a pair of youths caught my attention and brought me down to the nearby docks. The young men directed me to where a crowd gathered near Pier Four. My constable's badge and dragon's ash truncheon opened a path for me to the center of the assembled mass of humanity.

I could immediately see what had transformed their curiosity into general unruliness. A dark-skinned man lay on the pier in a growing pool of blood, a bloody longshoreman's hook on the wooden pier beside him.

The crowd seemed both fearful and disdainful of this man. I recognized him as a soldier under my commend from my days in the Royal Navy and moved in close to see what I could do.

I called him by name, James, and cradled his head in my lap, shocking many in the crowd. My memory was of a good sailor, strong swimmer, and fearless soldier.

James recognized me and grabbed my coat forcibly. He told me I had to find the boy, had to avenge this terrible act of bodily harm. I assured James that I would do everything in my power to bring about justice. There was little that could be done to save his life. The most I could do was make him comfortable.

James said that the scurrilous scamp stole from him. That they had agreed upon a price for the scrimshaw and the young man did not have enough money. The scrimshaw had not been easy to obtain and James wanted true value for his efforts.

James was attacked from behind by the honorless youth and gutted like some bottom feeder. Then the youth took the scrimshaw from him and ran.

James repeated this story several times as the Metropolitan Guard Crime Investigation Squad arrived with their arcane leather portmanteaus to gather evidence and do what they could to solve the crime.

James went still in my arms. He had expired.

Upon seeing James dead, the MGCIS stopped and conferred with each other. Then, they picked up the hook from the pier, stored it in one of their evidence bags, and left the scene.

I found it disgraceful that the MGCIS did nothing more than collect a single piece of evidence and leave without interviewing any of the crowd. All the same, with James expired, the crowd dispersed and went back to their everyday business.

I spent the remainder of my shift finding someone who would take James' body and ensure that it was interred properly. There was little to no hope of finding family but the least I could do was make sure his body wasn't left on the piers for the rats.

Upon returning to the station, my sergeant berated me for a full half hour for wasting time on dark scum when I could have been helping good citizens. I disagreed with the assessment of wasted time, but I kept my mouth shut.

⫯

Partial tarot deck of mixed provenance

Major Arcana 0 – The Fool - missing
Major Arcana I - The Magician - missing
Major Arcana II – Fire (Communication with the Dead Tarot Guild)

Major Arcana III – Water (Communication with the Dead Tarot Guild)

Major Arcana IV – Air (Communication with the Dead Tarot Guild)

Major Arcana V – Earth (Communication with the Dead Tarot Guild)

Major Arcana VI – The Lovers - missing

Major Arcana VII – The Chariot - missing

Major Arcana VIII – Equity (Health and Medicine Tarot Guild)

Major Arcana IX – Philosopher (Health and Medicine Tarot Guild)

Major Arcana X – Wheel of Fortune – cast in bronze and image etched deeply into its surface

Major Arcana XI – Strength - missing

Major Arcana XII – The Hanged Man - missing

Major Arcana XIII – Death - missing

Major Arcana XIV – Temperance - missing

Major Arcana XV – Illness (Communication with the Dead Tarot Guild)

Major Arcana XVI – The Tower - missing

Major Arcana XVII – Blood (Health and Medicine Tarot Guild)

Major Arcana XVIII – The Moon - carved from scrimshaw. When held one can hear crashing waves from the ocean.

Major Arcana XIX – Misery (Communication with the Dead Tarot Guild)

Major Arcana XX – Judgment – image tattooed on skin

of unknown mammal, perhaps human, attached to card-sized piece of dragon's ash.
Major Arcana XXI – The World – missing

- *Minor Arcana from Communication with the Dead Tarot (Pentacles and Cups; with exceptions noted below, only the Two, Five, Six, and Nine of Pentacles, and the Three, Six, and Eight of Cups were found with this deck)*
- *Minor Arcana from Battle Guild Tarot (Swords; with exceptions noted below, only the Two of Swords was found with the deck)*
- *Minor Arcana from Health and Medicine Guild (Wands; with exceptions noted below, only the Three, Five, and Six of Wands were found with this deck)*

Noted Exceptions:
- *Ace of Pentacles, Ace of Cups, Ace of Swords, and Ace of Wands – cards made of thin marble sheets with mother-of-pearl inlay. The card backs are blank.*
- *Three of Cups, Six of Wands, Nine of Pentacles, and Nine of Swords – cards made of dried sheets of seaweed with simple ink designs drawn on the front.*
- *Knave of Pentacles – card made of glass with exquisitely painted card front. The card back has repeating designs of pentacles etched into the glass surface.*
- *Knave of Cups – card is made of a delicate, thin piece of black shale; one of its corners is slightly crumbled.*

The card front looks blank. The card is identifiable due to its back having der Schurke der Tassen written on it in chalk.

- *Knave of Swords – card scorched as if set aflame; front and back damaged to the point where it is unable to determine the image on the front nor the design on the back.*
- *Knave of Wands – card is made of dragon's ash with design burned into the card front. The card back is blank.*

꒜

Interview of Graham Douglas, Captain of The Walpole
(conducted by Inspector Chauncey Gibb)
Friday August 7ᵗʰ, 1874

Chauncey Gibb: Can you tell me how you knew James Gough?

Graham Douglas: Guff? Is that how you pronounce it?

CG: *[pause]* I believe so.

GD: Well, I learn something new every day. That's how I stay so young! Always learning!

CG: And how did you know him?

GD: James was a sailor on *The Walpole*. Good sailor. Had Naval experience.

CG: Was it a problem that the man was dark skinned?

GD: Not for me, sir. Now, I don't like what you're implying, that he was mistreated just because of the color of his—

CG: Did his shipmates have issue with his skin color?

GD: No sir. If any did, I'd have them overboard before you can say spit. He was a Navy man! Lots of folks don't have that type of muster but James did. And I'll let you know, if he was good enough for His Majesty's Navy, he's more than good enough for me!

CG: Was it possible that someone on the crew resented his Naval past, maybe a crew member that couldn't pass the Naval exams?

[The record states that Graham Douglas paused before shaking his head.]

GD: Look, I'm not as much a fool as I appear. I'm sure there were men on the ship that had never worked with someone like James, but I tell you, he worked for me for two, three years. If there was problems with the crew, there's no way he would last that long.

CG: What kind of cargo does *The Walpole* carry?

GD: Nothing unusual. We start up the coast to the north, picking up lumber, whales, furs . . . the type of things you can't get down here. We head south, drop some cargo off, pick some up—textiles, wheat, corn, and the like—and then head further south. At the end we drop off the last of cargo from the north, some from around here, and pick up cotton, sugar, and such. Then we head back up coast making stops along the way. By the time we're back north again *The Walpole* is empty and sitting high in the water.

CG: No slaves or firearms?

GD: No sir. No illegal cargo. There's too much money to make with legitimate work.

CG: What do you know about Oliver Wolsey?

GD: That bastard. Killed one of my best sailors. I'd put a hook to him were he in front of me! Is he a big bloke?

CG: What? No, Wolsey is a youth. Barely over five feet tall.

GD: Huh. James was a big man. Tall for sure, I'm surprised Wolsey got the best of him.

CG: From what we can tell, Wolsey surprised him from behind. So you say you never met Wolsey?

GD: No. I wouldn't know the man if he was you.

CG: Any idea what Gough and he would have in common?

GD: James was a friend to the whalers up north. Did a tidy side business selling carved whale bone . . . scrimshaw? I suspect that bastard wanted some of that and James stood his ground on his price.

CG: You didn't care that one of your employees worked on the side?

GD: I don't allow sailors to do trade on *The Walpole* and they can't be looking to make an extra coin if there's still work to do. If their work is done, their time is their business. They know my work is good so they'll be back in the morning.

CG: If you think of anything else, please contact us.

GD: I will but don't sit up waiting for me.

⟿

Interview of Edgar Shipman, longshoreman in New Caldwell Seaport, member of The Hive union

(conducted by Inspector Chauncey Gibb)
Friday August 7th, 1874

Chauncey Gibb: Can you tell me how you knew James Gough?

Edgar Shipman: He's that darkskin that got killed the other night?

CG: He was. Yes.

ES: I knew of him. We didn't trade words.

CG: What about scrimshaw?

ES: I wouldn't touch anything from him if it came with a year's supply of golden pussy.

CG: Are you saying you did not like the man?

ES: I'm saying I don't know him. And I have no time for his type. The only way we'd talk is if he was in my way to the pub.

CG: So you wouldn't quarrel with the man?

ES: I don't start stuff. If he came at me, he should be prepared for a fight.

CG: From what I hear, the Hive is barely more than a gang of thugs ready to fight at the merest provocation. You're telling me someone like you who has a severe dislike of darkskinned people and is a proud member of the Hive wouldn't go out of your way to create problems for James Gough?

ES: *[silent for a long time]* We've been told to leave *The Walpole* and its crew alone. I won't say no more about it and that's more than you should hear.

CG: Did you know Oliver Wolsey?

ES: Agh. That little blighter was under everyone's feet. Always with the questions about the seaport and cargo and how we unload cargo. If you want to know about someone I would go out of my way to fuck with? That Wolsey is one.

CG: Where were you on the night of August 5th?

ES: Don't know. Drinking or fucking. That's all I do at night. Eventually I blackout and someone wakes me to come empty some cargo.

CG: So you weren't in the seaport when Wolsey attacked Gough?

ES: I wasn't on that pier, but I never really leave the seaport. To be honest inspector? I would've been just like the rest of the crowd if I was there. Standing and watching. Not helping. There's no money to be made in being kind to people.

CG: If you think of anything else, please contact us.

ES: Oh, no thank you, inspector.

[The record notes that shipman tore Inspector Gibb's card in half before departing.]

꒷

Interview – David Blokeman, proprietor of The Beautiful Lamp
(conducted by Inspector Chauncey Gibb)
Tuesday August 11th, 1874

David Blokeman: Are you here to help me with my claim of insurance?

Chauncey Gibb: Um, no. I'm with the Metropolitan Guard. Can you tell me how you knew Oliver Wolsey?

DB: Is that the name of the asshole that started a fucking fire and swung a fucking giant sword around? I've got notches in my joist work deep enough that I'm afraid to sleep upstairs!

CG: So you never met Wolsey before he entered your bar the other morning?

DB: No. Never saw the kid before. I thought about not letting him in but he had coin for a drink and coin wins over better judgment I guess.

CG: He hardly seems old enough to drink.

DB: As far as I know inspector there's no limit to how young you can be to taste a pint of ale. I've made the choice to not have kids of my own and then have to worry about bad choices they make, I'm certainly not going to worry about someone else's kids' bad choices.

CG: Did you notice anything unusual about Wolsey?

DB: Like I said, he was young and that always makes me suspicious. Then he kept fiddling with his damn tarot. They always make me nervous. I don't like Guild folk in my tavern and flashing cards around is one way to get the Guilds sniffing about.

CG: Why not ask him to leave?

DB: He had coin and was taking his sweet damn time finishing his beer. Probably the first time he ever tasted it and couldn't understand why everyone loves it so much.

CG: When did Constable Gurney arrive?

DB: Probably a few hours after Wolsey. I don't keep track of everyone but I suspect Gurney comes into The Lamp around eleven every day. He has lunch.

CG: Does he drink on the job?

DB: He has lunch.

CG: Did Gurney mention anything about Wolsey?

DB: Oh aye. We made a deep conversation about the lad. Wondering where his mother was and if we should take him in like a stray cat.

CG: There's no need for cheek my good man.

DB: Probably not, but that's what I have to give. Gurney saw him and asked a question or two about him. Unlike me, Gurney always needs to know why.

CG: When did you notice the Redhands?

DB: To be fair, I didn't. But in a bit, when Gurney heads over to Wolsey's table, he motions for a round of drinks. I see him looking toward the corner of the room, and that's when I saw 'em, but only because I felt like they wanted to be seen. Does that make sense?

CG: Some. What happened next?

DB: You see, my memory is a little fuzzy about that. I'm in back a lot because I'm preparing for the dock workers to come in after the ships are emptied and restocked. I was coming out front when it felt like the whole place is spinning like after the war when we all had too much drink.

CG: The floor was spinning?

DB: Not for real. It just felt like it was. As quickly as I feel it, it stops. I get out front to see what's happening and before I can round the corner of the bar, I hear shouting.

One of the Redhands is partway out the door but he's laying on the ground on fire. Wolsey has a great big sword in his hands. Gurney has his truncheon out, but he isn't getting too close to that blade. The other Red-hands is peeling cards off a deck and speaking quietly.

I think about heading right back into the kitchen when there's a bright flash of light. So bright it near blinded me. I can't really speak to what happened.

I heard Gurney shouting that Wolsey should put down his sword and back up against the wall. Wolsey was shouting something about not letting the Redhands take him alive. There was a lot of other noise but nothing I could make out.

By the time my eyes cleared up, there was just Gurney in the bar talking to some inspectors. The Redhands were gone. Wolsey was gone.

CG: Thank you. You've been very helpful. If you think of anything else, please contact us.

DB: I will. If you see an insurer out and about, send them here.

⊃–∘

Hand-copied transcript of Constable Marcus Gurney's journal, entry dated August 11th

I met Oliver Wolsey yesterday, murderer of former Lance Corporal James Gough, and more importantly, someone I considered a friend. At first, I did not know who he was or I would have worked to apprehend him on the spot.

The Sergeant had shared his name out before the con-stables were released to their beats. I had a name and the vaguest description. He could have been any number of youths I pass on a daily basis.

As it was, I entered The Beautiful Lamp yesterday midday for my standard meal and pint. I noted a youth sitting a table with a mostly full pint glass playing with an unusual deck of cards. Initially I was not aware that they were tarot.

David, the proprietor, already had my pint on the bar and I knew the food would be coming shortly. I liked to get in before the dock workers finished up unloading and loading ships at the seaport. The Lamp got loud and disorderly and I liked a bit of quiet. It also didn't make sense to spend a lot of time breaking up fights and arguments when it was just men blowing off steam. If I was there as a member of the Metropolitan Guard, it would behoove me to uphold the law which would not endear me to anyone.

I asked James about the young man and he mentioned that the youth was at the front door when he opened up for the day. The youth had coin and the bar was empty. James would chase him out when the dock workers arrived.

I ate my meal—some delicious fried fish and potatoes—but kept an eye on the young man. At that moment it was clear to me that he was working with a tarot deck and not one of the gambling decks James kept behind the bar for the workers.

The young man played a few cards from a Diviners tarot, which was odd as he was not dressed in the Diviners Guild vestments. It varied from guild to guild, but in general the guilds did not like outsiders using their cards.

I went to put more fish in my mouth and almost missed when the next card he placed was from the Battle Tarot Guild. I had never heard of someone blending decks. I decided to have a word with the young man.

I was finishing my pint when he laid out a card carved from scrimshaw. When the card hit the table, it glowed softly. There was no chance that was a coincidence. He fit the description from the Sergeant and the scrimshaw settled it for me: this was my suspect.

I set down my empty glass and readied myself to walk over when he pulled a cream-colored card with a single red handprint on its back and set it into his tableau. What I had taken for a nervous tick of looking towards the door was now clearly the young man keeping an eye on the pair sitting in a dark corner of the tavern.

Their red vestments were so dark I hadn't noticed them at first, but there were two members of the Health and Medicine Tarot Guild watching the young man.

Known as Redhands, the Health and Medicine Tarot Guild definitely did not allow their cards to be handled by anyone outside their guild. How Oliver came to possess such cards was beyond my imagination.

I knew it was imperative to apprehend Oliver, not just to hold him accountable for the murder of James Gough, but to protect him from the Health and Medicine Tarot Guild. If they got their hands on him, James' killer would never see justice.

I moved to Oliver's table and he tried to get me to leave him alone. I appealed to his wellbeing and good judgment to get him out of the tavern safely. Oliver scoffed and said that he could take care of himself.

I took a different tack and said that I didn't want my favorite tavern getting busted up in whatever was going to happen between him and the guild members in the corner.

Oliver didn't answer; he just pulled an over-sized card from his deck whose back was covered in elephants and crocodiles. I wasn't sure which guild those cards were from. Then he smiled at me—the cheek of this youth!—and drew a card that looked like polished bronze and set it in the center of his tableau. A Wheel of Fortune was etched delicately into the card's front.

When he placed it, it appeared that the cards were floating above, beneath, and in the table. As I watched, the table appeared to revolve slowly and I had to grip its sides to keep from falling out of my chair.

I tried to speak, but my mind was busy trying to keep from sliding away. The entire floor felt like it was tipping slowly and that I was certain to crash down into it before too long.

Oliver swept the cards up and shuffled his deck with a giggle and the room stopped moving.

I had to get this situation under control.

I called him kid and Oliver corrected me with his full name. One of the two Redhands stood and left the tavern quickly. I shouted for him to stop but he kept going.

Oliver shuffled the deck rapidly but I could tell his attention was on the remaining Redhands. I looked over and saw the guild member was shuffling his own deck.

He moved rapidly.

He stood and swung his right hand forward in one motion. A huge flash of light nearly blinded me. I could see indistinct shapes, but nothing more.

As my eyes cleared up, I saw Oliver push himself back from the table, put his hands together, and pulled a long glowing sword from somewhere. A smoldering card fell to the table.

The guild member threw another card at Oliver and he blocked it with his sword and rushed the guild member who stood stock still, clearly not expecting Oliver to be able to fight back.

Neither had been trained to fight as I had. I was between them before either knew I was moving. I met Oliver's sword with my truncheon which stopped the sword, but it bit into the wood which should not have been possible.

The Redhands threw another card but this one exploded into a thick cloud of smoke when it struck the floor. I was trying to wrest the sword from Oliver's hands and therefore wasn't able to stop this guild member either. I could smell burning as the smoke did not clear.

Oliver's sword hit my truncheon a second time but turned into mist. Because I was pressing so hard against the sword, when it disappeared I toppled to the floor. Before I could regain my feet, Oliver was over me and out the door.

I worked with Blokeman to get the fire out.

My superior insisted that Oliver must have had the sword on him and that I merely missed it. I agreed that he was correct. But we both knew that magic was a thing that happened in New Caldwell even if the official Metropolitan Guard line was to deny its existence. That was absurd as members of all the Mage Unions worked within the Metropolitan Guard departments.

᠀—

Communication with the Dead Tarot Guild Board Meeting August 13th, 1874

Board Members in Attendance
Ford Xavier (President)
Gregory Fullmore (Vice-President)
Sid Fawns (Secretary)
Roscoe Matson (Treasurer)
Gerald Collins
Ignatius Howlett
Emmet Norman
Richard Purcell
Bryan Potter
Percival Xavier
Board Members Not in Attendance
Elder Cook
Virgil Gleeson
Benedict Smith
Orrin Skidd.

1.　　Call to Order
Chair called meeting to order at eight o'clock in the evening of the thirteenth of August, 1874.

2.   Approval of Agenda

ON A MOTION MADE by Howlett, SECONDED by Potter and CARRIED, the agenda was approved as circulated.

3.   Conflict of Interest

None.

4.   Approval of Previous Minutes

ON A MOTION DULY MADE by Collins SECONDED by Howlett and CARRIED the draft minutes of the Guild's meeting of the seventeenth of July were approved as presented.

5.   Old Business

a.   Membership Dues

Treasurer Matson read off a list of members who still needed to pay their dues. He reminded all those present that the Guild could not run itself as a business and be considered a serious Guild if they did not have the funds owed from members. All members of the Guild were vetted prior to being allowed and as such, the Guild knew that everyone could afford the dues.

President Xavier MADE A MOTION that dues needed to be paid before the next meeting or membership would be revoked. MOTION SECONDED by Howlett and CARRIED in a unanimous vote.

b.   Vestments

Treasurer Matson reported that new vestments had arrived from the tailor and were available for all fully paid members.

6. New Business

a. Oliver Wolsey

Ignatius Howlett wanted to bring to the Guild's attention that there was a young man going about New Caldwell brazenly using cards from multiple Guilds. Howlett had it on good authority that this Wolsey character held multiple Communication with the Dead Tarot cards and thought the board should launch an investigation into how Wolsey obtained the cards.

Purcell MOVED that the board form an investigatory committee which was SECONDED by Howlett and CARRIED in a unanimous vote.

b. Membership Dues Increase

Treasurer Matson indicated that the board should consider raising dues if it was going to continue its push for new members. The Guildhall was a historical building in a prime area, and those costs were not going to go down in the future.

Additionally, the tarot cards were quite expensive to manufacture and since the board was unwilling to change the materials used in card manufacture, those costs had to be covered somewhere.

President Xavier clarified that board was not going to move the Guildhall to a new location as it was a major reason that attracted new members and members of the public looking for its services. President Xavier further explained that it wasn't just merely being unwilling to change the cards structure, but that they were unable to because changing the materials used to manufacture the cards would render them unusable for the Guild's activities in communicating with the dead.

President Xavier TABLED discussion on this matter for the next meeting.

7.   Committee Reports

MEMBERSHIP COMMITTEE reported that they had ten new members ready for vetting. Treasurer Matson questioned if it was sensible to be increasing membership numbers so rapidly.

President Xavier explained that if the Guild wanted to compete with the Prophets of the Unknown, then increasing its numbers was the only way.

Howlett MADE A MOTION to have the potential candidates vetted and invited to the next meeting. MOTION SECONDED by President Xavier and CARRIED unanimously.

No other committees met since the last meeting.

8.   Staff Reports

None.

9.   Adjournment

ON A MOTION MADE by Howlett, SECONDED by Purcell and CARRIED, the meeting was adjourned at nine o'clock.

꒖

Interview of [NAME REDACTED], member of Health and Medi-
cine Tarot Guild
(Conducted by Inspector Chauncey Gibb)
Friday August 14th, 1874

Chauncey Gibb, Inspector: How did the Health and
Medicine Tarot Guild become aware of Oliver Wolsey?

[NAME REDACTED]: He was invited to a board meeting by [**REDACTED**]. I understand he was to petition to
become a member.

CG: Does your Guild take on a lot of new members?

[NR]: [**REDACTED**]

CG: So it was unusual for Wolsey to actually attend a
meeting to request becoming a member?

[NR]: Yes, very much so.

CG: Was there ever any serious thought given to listening
to his plea?

[NR]: No.

CG: How did Wolsey appear at the meeting? Was he
nervous? Excited?

[NR]: [**REDACTED**]

CG: One could surmise that Wolsey would be disap-
pointed to give up his time to attend a purposeless meeting. He could even reasonably be angry at his treatment.

[NR]: The Health and Medicine Tarot Guild is not a
social club. If Wolsey did the research he purported to
have done, he would know before attending the meeting
that the chance of him successfully becoming a member
was essentially zero.

CG: So why bother?

[NR]: You would have to ask him that.

CG: We will.

[NR]: So the Metropolitan Guard has him in custody?

CG: I cannot comment on the status of our investigation. What was the Guild's reaction when you learned that Wolsey was using tarot from your Guild without permission?

[NR]: [**REDACTED**]

CG: I'm surprised you would admit that to a member of the Metropolitan Guard.

[NR]: [**REDACTED**]

CG: Sir, I'm confident in our investigation. The Guild should step aside and let the proper authorities handle this matter.

[NR]: [**REDACTED**]

CG: Thank you sir. You have my card should you need to reach me.

>—∘

Interview of Ignatius Howlett, member of Communication with the Dead Tarot Guild
(Conducted by Inspector Chauncey Gibb)
Friday August 14th, 1874

Chauncey Gibb: How did the Communication with the Dead Tarot Guild become aware of Oliver Wolsey?

Ignatius Howlett: Some of our agents, Guild staff you know, reported to us that there was a young man, recently arrived to New Caldwell, that was flashing an unusual tarot deck to anyone who wanted to see. It was Wolsey, and he had cards from our tarot, which isn't allowed.

CG: Does the Guild do anything to enforce who has access to your tarot?

IH: We have very strict ordinances in place to regulate who can enter and exit the facilities where our tarot are made. At least I thought we had strict ordinances in place. We are an exclusive Guild, not for just any member of society. No, we are made up of the best, the highest members of society. It irks me to no end that this wastrel was able to steal Tarot from us.

CG: So how would Wolsey have gone about obtaining your Tarot?

IH: I honestly have no idea. I suspect some member of our staff feels underpaid or some such nonsense and took money from this ragamuffin for a handful of tarot. You see, to most people I suspect their understanding is so lacking that the tarot appear as nothing more than glorified playing cards, but they are much more than that.

CG: Your staff understands the tarot? Understands the power of the cards?

IH: Under my oversight, staff was fully vetted prior to hiring. Background checks, references, sponsorship by members . . .

But now that my talents are needed elsewhere in the Guild I suspect that all is lacking now and Potter and Xavier—Percival Xavier, not President Xavier—are doing a right shoddy job of hiring staff.

CG: Is it possible that Wolsey stole the cards?

IH: I'd actually prefer to learn that he stole them rather than obtaining them through some malfeasance by staff. We've created an investigatory committee to look into the matter.

CG: Excellent. I'll give you my card so you can provide us with any new information you feel is relevant.

IH: Of course. And here is my card in case you need to ask any more questions. I'm always more than happy to talk about the Guild.

Hand-copied transcript of Constable Marcus Gurney's journal, entry dated Sunday August 16th

The Nine Points is a difficult place to investigate crime. Gang activity makes residents reluctant to talk in the best of times. Now I needed to find someone in the Nine Points who was playing with fire as far as the Tarot Guilds were concerned and I doubted whether I could find anyone willing to talk.

I left word for my typical informants that I was trying to locate Wolsey. Normally they needed a day or two to gather information and that was time I did not have. It was a long shot to ask them for help, but I had to try everything I could.

I wandered in and out of the typical places criminals went to when trying to lay low, but there was no sign of Wolsey and everyone refused to talk to me.

I was too well known and it was too well known what I wanted.

I stood at an empty street corner thinking about my next move. Any other night I would have to watch out for fast-moving carriages, street toughs, magicians, street walkers, and even the occasionally higher-class person looking for something out of the ordinary.

The fact that the streets were empty was a bad sign. I figured my best hope would be to find Wolsey's body.

Something prodded me in the back and a rough voice told me not to turn around. The voice gave me a recent location of Wolsey and encouraged me to hurry.

Wolsey's room at the New Caldwell Youth Association was essentially bare. There were few affects and little in the way of belongings.

Wolsey was gone. I held little hope of getting another tip to his whereabouts. But sometimes luck is on your side.

On a side table was a stack of tarot cards. I picked them up and put them in my pocket. There was a scrap of paper on the table and when I picked it up it was an attempt at forgery for a ticket on a ship heading south.

I headed to the seaport as fast as I could. I doubted I would find Wolsey on the ship scrawled on the fake ticket now in my pocket, but again, I had to follow what leads I had.

When I arrived at the dock in question, the ship was already away from the pier and heading out to sea.

It was too far to be certain, but I would swear an oath that standing at the stern of the boat was Wolsey. He was waving to me. If I squinted, I could imagine a smile on his face.

He had gotten away but he could never return. New Caldwell was now closed to him. If he ever came back, I would likely only learn about it because he was in the morgue.

As Big as a Whale

~ *Avra Margariti*

1

The astronomer's second wife called her husband *Darling* and *Dearest*. Their boy—three and a half vibrant years, two dimples, one missing front tooth—called him *Father*. The gargantuan whale circling their galactic observation tower expels echolocation groans across starlit dark matter, splashing with languid intent over the astronomer's sonogram sensors. Through the lens of his telescope, her sight etches itself in silver thread onto his retinas. The whale doesn't acknowledge the astronomer. He is but a cosmic speck on her back that has borne millennia of creation and destruction.

Ever since the marble orrery which contained the astronomer's second wife and son was swallowed by the whale, nobody calls the astronomer anything in his empty tower amidst the half-known universe.

He's called the whale his nemesis long before that.

☉

2

The whale isn't gray or black or even white. She swims through deep space and shadow matter, a rainbowed shimmer clinging to her thick skin, like nacre or the underside of Jupiter's rings.

The astronomer holes himself up in his highest tower, surrounded by astrolabes and vellum scrolls. The observatory—resembling a black-stone keep—is held aloft through an esoteric blend of science and alchemy. His old laboratory in the west wing lies in shambles, the reinforced glass shattered, half of his instruments obliterated under the whale's menace. Delirious, he contorts his spine over his new journals, scribbles of squid ink only he can read, while his tea grows death-cold and gibbous moons of mold sprout from his toast.

Hypothesis: The whale is the keeper of all the secrets of the universe.

He turns a page and watches his pen wobble. *It's a wicked world in all meridians.* He doesn't remember writing this.

A bellow sounds from outside, deep and velvet matte, high-pitched and silky silver. The bellow encompasses everything the universe has to offer. The whale does, too. The astronomer often wonders about what he'd find if he could dissect her. Just a tiny, tender piece. He bruises his eyes against his telescope, catching flicks of the whale's dorsal fin, her flippers, her tail flukes. They leave comet trails of stardust behind them. Tainting the sky, taunting him forevermore.

Blindly, the astronomer extends a hand to his left, expecting the orrery's smooth planets within easy reach, to stroke and whisper to them, *soon, soon the whale will be captured and you shall be free.*

But the marble orrery is gone, last he saw it caught between the needle-sharp, turret-sized teeth of the whale. The astronomer's hand knocks his tea over.

- 3

The astronomer is also an astrophant: someone who reveals the sacred secrets of stars. He shoots tridents and harpoons from his observation deck. Sixth-magnitude stars are the dimmest, therefore easiest to catch. He reels them in, spreads them out under his scalpel and microscope. His harpoon gun, however, is far too small and flimsy for his great, cosmic archenemy. He attempts to order a bigger weapon from the space pirates that roam this part of the galaxy. When he cannot strike a deal—when even the back-stabbing mercenaries blanch at the thought of crossing the whale—the astronomer decides to build his own device.

Yet his meticulous notes and designs, his formulas and measurements, always end up ink-smudged or vanished altogether come morning. Sometimes he suspects his wife and son, although he's never caught them in the act.

Other times, he thinks they'd never disobey him. Not like his first, wilful wife, eaten by the whale some years ago. Perhaps this floating observatory is haunted by ghosts after all.

- 2

The whale dances, but sings also. He's recorded the frequency of the wavelengths but has had no luck decoding them. At least not when the song is directed toward the abstract vastness of the cosmos. When the astronomer's wife brings his lunch to his laboratory, the whale's song shifts, the sonogram spiking. The second wife pauses, plate-laden tray held aloft, as the echolocation music morphs into a sea shanty. Certain passages almost resemble a mating call. When the astronomer's son visits his father for a goodnight kiss on his sweaty, salty forehead, the song mellows into a lullaby.

The second wife often sleeps in the boy's bed, cradling him in dreams, nautili in their shells. Alone in his tower, the astronomer sends recordings of himself, like harpoons, out into the universe. He tries to communicate with the whale that stole his first wife, but her response resounds with flat apathy rather than its customary polyphony. If there are traces of anger woven through the rumbling notes, it's the type of anger a person experiences toward an incessantly buzzing mosquito.

The astronomer detests this. He can take being hated, but he cannot abide being ignored.

3

Dust gathers over every surface. The astronomer places it under his microscope to ascertain it's not made of the stars swirling outside his window, or ghosts. Then again, everything is stars. Everywhere he looks are ghosts.

Dishes pile in the sink. The stone dulls, the tower falls into disrepair. When not a single crumb remains, the astronomer is forced to call the intergalactic delivery company for supplies. He stands in the doorway, oxygen mask secured haphazardly over his face, when his order arrives. He prefers when it's a little robot bringing the groceries. The flesh-and-bone delivery boy cannot hide his surprise at the sight of the astronomer: his ink-stained robe and weeks-old facial hair, the dark circles and glazed over eyes.

"Doctor," the boy says, collecting himself. "I trust your wife and son are well?"

"Hmm?" The astronomer peers over the boy's shoulders, but the whale is gone. Only the boy's enchanted velocipede hovers obediently behind him. "Oh, them. The whale got them."

Unlike the last times anyone inquired after his wife and son, the astronomer doesn't have to lie.

The delivery boy's eyes widen to the size of moons behind his mask. "Doctor! Should I talk to the men at the fuel station? Arrange a hunt?"

The astronomer shuts the door in the boy's slack face. "No need. The whale is mine."

-1

The second wife isn't as young or pretty as the first, but she's good at what she does. As she cleans the observatory to a black-diamond shine and washes their clothes and linens, she sings sea shanties of old. While hearty stews simmer on the stove, she recites poetry, likening the observatory to a lighthouse and, more and more lately, a floating prison. She walks through the halls like an echo, wielding her feather duster as a maestro's baton. Sometimes she pauses, head tilted, listening to strains of ghosts. She always picks the sweetest songs and saddest poems when the ghosts are listening.

Reach me down my Tycho Brahe, I would know him when we meet.

The astronomer bristles and blazes like an imploding star. This was his first wife's favorite poem. "Where did you find it?" he demands, but his second wife only blinks. The astronomer tears the tower apart but finds no book of poetry. From then on, he prohibits songs and poems of any kind.

The astronomer's son has never seen the sunlight. Day and night, the world outside remains unchanging in its blackness. It might be cruel raising him here, but the astronomer believes you cannot miss what you've never known. The boy sprints up and down the spiral staircases, banging sticks and toys against frigid stone. When his toys are taken away, he takes to slamming himself against the walls. His arms and legs at first, then his head. Each heavy thud, each string of toddler talk, drives migrainous holes deeper into the astronomer's skull as he hunches over his formulas. He needs to know things, and to know things he needs to study the whale, and to study the whale he needs to capture it, and his first wife with it. But to do all that, he needs silence above all.

"I'm working," he shouts. "Make him stop, or I'll do it."

But even when the wife and son fall quiet, a paranoid part of him thinks they're still communicating. It's the way stars talk to one another, on nearly untraceable wavelengths. Echolocation, the whale's cosmic language he has yet to decipher.

The astronomer leaves his laboratory in a flurry of white robes. Throbbing headache and unfurling fury, he searches the tower for his wife and their undisciplined son. He finds her at their bedroom's window, body locked in a swaying dance, eyes fogged over. Her hands roam hypnotic over her own body, mouth opening and closing in soundless motifs. The whale is outside, swimming tight circles, opening and closing her great maws.

"Do you talk to her?" the astronomer asks, clutching his wife's upper arms with bruising strength. "What lies is she spewing?"

"Let me go," his second wife says.

He doesn't.

Somewhere in the distance, his son wails and bellows.

☉

-4

The astronomer's first wife was young and beautiful, and eaten by the whale. That's what he told his second wife, and what she in turn told their son.

The astronomer lies, yet the astronomer remembers.

How the first wife walked out of the the tower and into the universe without an oxygen mask, her unshod feet barely touching the floor, her pearly mouth shaping the familiar lines of an old poem.

I have sworn, like Tycho Brahe, that a greater man may reap.

The astronomer watched from his laboratory, too late to run, too curious to stop her.

The first wife—so young, so beautiful—moved like a ghost in her white, gauzy gown woven with starlight. It billowed out around her calves, stretching taut over her half-moon belly growing fuller by the day. She walked down the boardwalk of the floating keep, while the whale's perennial dance changed from a solo to a pas-de-deux. At the end of the boardwalk the whale awaited; its mouth wide open, teeth glittering with secrets. The first wife curtsied before stepping so gracefully, so eagerly, into the mouth of the whale.

☉

0

The astronomer's second wife cried *Darling, no, Dearest, please* when he discovered the alchemy that would trap her inside the marble orrery. His son wailed *fatherfatherfather* when he joined his mother in their own miniature Venus, set like a a paperweight upon the astronomer's desk.

"You'll be safe here," the astronomer tells them, stroking the curved glass as they pound against it from the inside. "Away from the whale."

They'll be safe and protected, and he will be free of nuisance and distraction, left to do his sacred work undisturbed.

When the whale swims to his laboratory's window like a silent, hulking ship, the astronomer is too absorbed in his research to notice. He looks up in time to see her giant tail slam against the glass magicked to withstand the pressure of outer space. It smashes into a thousand tiny pieces. The astronomer doesn't have time to reach for a mask or a harpoon. He's never seen the whale without glass separating them. Her eye is bigger than a black hole. It brings all the fears of humanity to the surface. *I've been here before you*, it says, *and I will remain after you're nothing but stardust, and after the dust eats itself, regurgitating a new universe.*

The astronomer gasps from the lack of oxygen and the plethora of knowledge. When the whale opens her mouth to snatch the marble Venus containing the astronomer's wife and son, he can do nothing but scream. The whale cradles the marble carefully between her rictus smile. Then, she's gone.

The astronomer remains in the glass wreckage for a long while, puffing into an oxygen mask, intoxicated by the eldritch encounter and his own fury.

4

The astronomer sits at his desk, writing, despairing. All his experiments fail, all his hypotheses prove weak and foolish. The view is dim through his magnifying glass, the ink bleeds illegible through his parchments. He's heard of planets where people's sins manifest as demons, stuck like humps on their owners' backs, bending them in half with the weight of guilt. A poet might have claimed the whale is one such manifestation. The astronomer never did like poetry.

Even stronger than the guilt is the righteous anger. Anger that his wife and son will learn everything the whale hid—all the secrets of the universe revealed from the inside out—and he won't. He pictures his first and second wife meeting in the belly of the beast. They orbit each other in mistrust at first, then gravitate closer and closer together. They fall in love, familiar ghosts engaged in a long-awaited dance. They paint constellations against the whale's walls, figures and formulas the astronomer can never dream of. The two former wives raise his children together, all four of them speaking in echolocation, the language of whales and stars.

Celestial bodies dance outside his window, and the whale does too. The astronomer sleeps in his dusty bed, with his dirty clothes and empty stomach. He sleeps, and he fears the starlit night.

CONTRIBUTORS

Marilee Dahlman

Marilee lives in Washington, DC, where she writes fiction first thing in the morning and works as a lawyer for the rest of the day. Her other stories have appeared in *Apparition Lit*, *The Bitter Oleander*, *Cleaver*, *Metaphorosis*, *Orca Lit,* and elsewhere.

She can be found on Twitter @marilee_dahlman.

Rhonda Eikamp

Rhonda Eikamp grew up in Texas and now lives in Germany, land of dark fairy tales and fast highways. Her short stories have appeared in a variety of venues, including *Lightspeed*, *Lackington's*, *Nightscript*, and *The Dark*. When not writing fiction, she translates for a German law firm and does Tarot readings for friends with her Salvador Dali deck.

Some of her stories may be found at her blog: https://writingin-thestrangeloop.wordpress.com/stories/

Nina Kiriki Hoffman

Over the past four decades, Nina Kiriki Hoffman has sold adult and young adult novels and more than 350 short stories. Her works have been finalists for the World Fantasy, Mythopoeic,

Sturgeon, Philip K. Dick, and Endeavour awards. Her novel *The Thread that Binds the Bones* won a Horror Writers Association Stoker Award, and her short story "Trophy Wives" won a Science Fiction & Fantasy Writers of America Nebula Award.

Nina does production work for the *The Magazine of Fantasy & Science Fiction.* She teaches short story classes through Lane Community College, Wordcrafters in Eugene, and Fairfield County Writers' Studio. She lives in Eugene, Oregon.

For a list of Nina's publications, check out: http://ofearna.us/books/hoffman.html.

John Klima

John Klima previously worked in New York's publishing jungle before returning to school to earn his Master's in Library Science. He now works full time as the Technology Manager of a large public library. John edited and published the Hugo Award-winning genre zine *Electric Velocipede* from 2001 to 2013.

When he is not conquering the world of indexing, John writes short stories and novels. He and his family live in the Midwest.

Avra Margariti

Avra Margariti is a queer author and poet from Greece. Avra's work haunts publications such as *Vastarien*, *Baffling Magazine*, *Strange Horizons*, *Lackington's*, *Best Microfiction*, and *Best Small Fictions*.

You can find Avra on twitter (@avramargariti).

Jordan Taylor

Jordan Taylor's short fiction has recently appeared in *Uncanny* and *The Deadlands*, and was nominated for a 2021 World Fantasy Award. Though she's lived in cities across the US, she's finally settled in North Carolina in a little cottage full of books.

You can follow her online at jordantaylorwrites.com, or on Twitter @JordanRTaylor13.

PAMELA COLMAN SMITH

The tarot images in this issue of Arcana are from the deck illustrated by Pamela Colman Smith. It was released in 1909 as the Rider-Waite deck (so named, at that time, in reference to its publisher, William Rider & Son). It remains the most influential and widely used tarot deck. While the impetus for the deck came from Arthur Edward Waite, Colman Smith was responsible for the iconography of the cards.

Pamela Colman Smith also illustrated over twenty books, wrote two collections of Jamaican folklore, edited two magazines, and ran the Green Sheaf Press, a small press devoted to women writers. She continued to write and illustrate throughout her life.

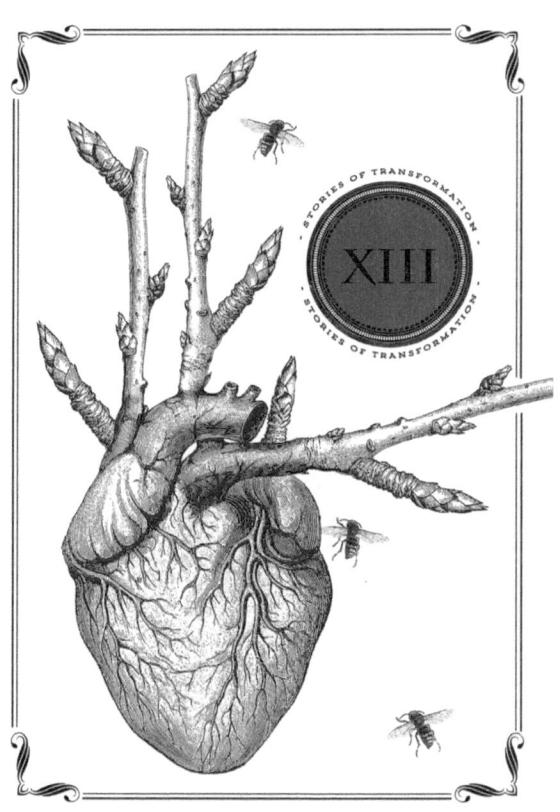

STORIES OF TRANSFORMATION

XIII

STORIES OF TRANSFORMATION

XIII

The thirteenth Tarot card is Death, and he is a symbol not of the end, but of transformation and rebirth. This is the genesis and root of *Thirteen: Stories of Transformation.* The twenty-eight authors of this collection are voices—new and old—who are not afraid to explore what comes next. Whether it be a life after death, a life without love, a life filled with hunger, or the life shared by a ghost. These are stories of the weird, the mythic, the fantastic, the futuristic, the supernatural, and the horrific.

With stories by Liz Argall • M. David Blake • Richard Bowes • George Cotronis • Amanda C. Davis • Julie C. Day • Jetse de Vries • Jennifer Giesbrecht • Daryl Gregory • Rik Hoskin • Rebecca Kuder • Claude Lalumière • Marc Levinthal • Grá Linnaea • Alex Dally MacFarlane • Juli Mallett • Lyn McConchie • Fiona Moore • Gregory L. Norris • Adrienne J. Odasso • Cat Rambo • Andrew Penn Romine • David Tallerman • Tais Teng Richard Thomas • Fran Wilde • A. C. Wise • Christie Yant

Edited by Mark Teppo.

Available at independent bookstores everywhere.

http://www.underlandpress.com

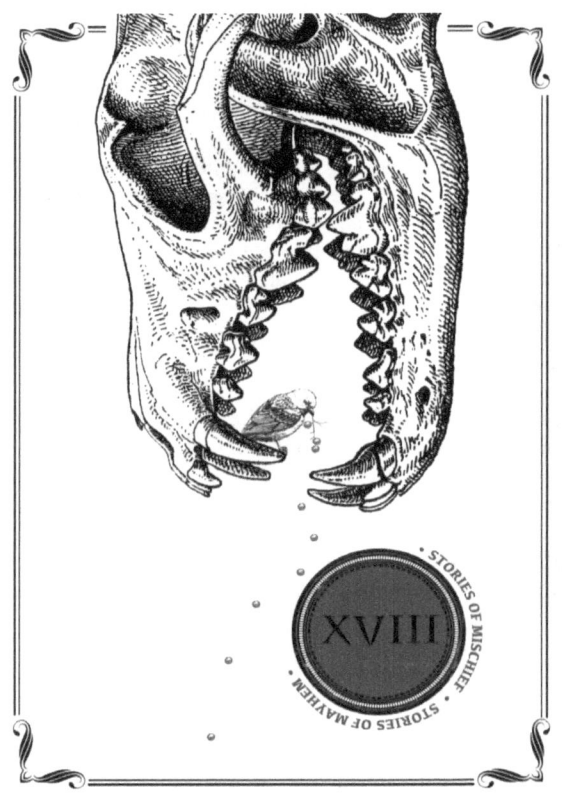

· STORIES OF MISCHIEF ·

XVIII

· STORIES OF MAYHEM ·

XVIII

The eighteenth Tarot card is the Moon, and those who raise their arms to her know she offers Mercy and Severity in equal measure. This is the great river at night, where wolves howl and all doors are open. All futures are possible, and every truth is elusive. This is the source and passion of *Eighteen: Stories of Mischief & Mayhem*. These twenty-four stories from voices—old and new—celebrate the inevitability of fate, the horror of prophecy, and the shivering delight of not knowing what comes next.

Cross over the threshold with us, and explore the strange, the weird, and the fantastic. Do not fear what lies ahead. It is the same as what came before. The only difference is you. This is *Eighteen*, and nothing will be the same.

With stories by Forrest Aguirre • Darin Bradley • Christopher East • Scott Edelman • Nicole Feldringer • Ben Gamblin • Ingrid Garcia • A. P. Howell • Emma Johnson-Rivard • E. E. King • Jessie Kwak • Shannon Lawrence • Gerri Leen • Mark Mills • Christi Nogle Tammie Painter • Josh Rountree • Erica Sage • Lorraine Schein • J. Dee Stanley • Richard Thomas • John Waterfall • Wendy N. Wagner • Todd Zack

Edited by Mark Teppo.

Available at independent bookstores everywhere.

http://www.underlandpress.com